CHARLES AND ELIZABETH

CHARLES AND ELIZABETH

A NOVEL

by

W. J. BURLEY

WALKER AND COMPANY
NEW YORK

First published in the United States of America
in 1981 by the Walker Publishing Company, Inc.

ISBN: 0-8027-5447-3

Library of Congress Catalog Card Number: 81-51973

Printed in the United States of America

10 9 8 7 6 5 4 3 2 1

CHAPTER ONE

'IT MIGHT DO the trick, Brian—an emotional catharsis. At any rate it's worth a try. After all, we've nothing to lose.'

Your modern institutional psychiatrist no longer looks and sounds like a shaman who has been to Oxford; he is often boisterously friendly, calls you by your first name and talks to you as though you were only slightly retarded. He lets you know 'quite frankly' that he is not a miracle worker, that he has doubts about the nature of your problem and his techniques, and in taking you into his confidence he undermines yours.

'Let it all go, get it down on paper, and when you've done that we'll look at it together.'

'May I have my typewriter brought in?'

'Of course.' He smiled, showing a lot of teeth through his red beard, and looked at the telephone, hoping that it would ring, then at the door, hoping that it would open. Frustrated on both counts he sighed and said, 'Well, Brian, see you on Thursday—that is, unless you have anything special you want to talk to me about in the meantime . . . By the way, how's the group therapy working out? . . . I know!—don't tell me, it's not your scene. Never mind, it's worth pegging away. Try everything and perhaps, one day, who knows?'

So this is a therapeutic exercise prescribed by the psychiatrist who is responsible for me in this institution which was once a lunatic asylum, then a mental hospital, and is now simply, if equivocally, a hospital. I am what is known as a 'voluntary patient', which means that I can walk out if I want to, but if I do I have no job for I have been told that I may not return to teaching until I have received 'satisfactory treatment'.

5

The problem is that I am supposed to have seen visions and dreamed dreams, in other words that I have suffered hallucinations. Society has never been comfortable with such people, and has always treated them with a certain ambivalence. Many have been burned at the stake, others have been canonized, while a few have been burned first and then canonized. Nowadays we are merely cases for treatment.

Certainly I have strange experiences, but my view of them, which is quite different from that of the psychiatrists, will emerge along with the facts.

It all began on Easter Monday afternoon when I was looking at the village church of St Martin-in-Powder. It is a spartan, chunky, satisfying little building on the outside, typically Cornish, but the inside has been spoiled by a nineteenth-century restoration which has left very little that is worth looking at. Stained glass, pews, pulpit, font and reredos are all unashamedly and dolefully Victorian.

I put my conscience money in the box and was on the point of leaving when I noticed a little pile of leaflets held down by a hymn book and a notice: *Antiquities of the Parish of St Martin-in-Powder—15p.*

The leaflet comprised several pages of duplicated typescript and two or three poorly reproduced sketches. Most of the text was devoted to the church and its history, but there were notes on the village inn, some seventeenth-century almshouses, and Tregear House. I am interested in the Stuart period, and it was the date of Tregear House which caught my eye.

Built in 1700 for Edward Bottrell, Tregear House is a splendid example of a small country house in the Queen Anne or Late Stuart style. The front door with its 'shell' canopy is particularly fine, and inside the house the oak panelling of the drawing-room and the plaster ceilings of both drawing-room and library are well worth seeing. The house is built at the head of a combe and ornamental gardens, about thirty acres in extent, run down to the sea at Penwithick Cove. The gardens are notable for many varieties of camellia, for a waterfall, and for a large maze.

A sketch, unevenly printed, showed a typical Queen Anne house with a terrace, set in a park with sheep grazing in the foreground. The caption read: 'Reproduced from a nineteenth-century water-colour by kind permission of Arthur Clark Esq.'

The text went on to give a few details of the Bottrell family.

The Bottrells claimed descent from William de Botreaux, a fourteenth-century lord of north Cornwall. During the eighteenth century they acquired large interests in the mining and smelting of tin, and in 1801 Joseph Bottrell of Tregear founded the banking house of Bottrell, Clyma and Rogers, which prospered until it was absorbed by one of the national banks in 1900. The last member of the Bottrell family to live at Tregear, Miss Amelia Clark-Bottrell, died in 1970 at the great age of one hundred and one, and since her death the house has remained un-tenanted.

The village of St Martin-in-Powder is a mile and a half inland from Veryan Bay, and Tregear lies between it and the sea. I left the Mini parked by the churchyard wall and set off down a narrow lane which, because of the elms arching over it, was more like a tunnel. The hedges were mossy, sprouting young ferns and clumps of primroses. After five minutes' walking the lane widened, and to my left there was a white gate set between impressive granite posts, and beyond it an overgrown drive. Through the trees I could just see the house, a glimpse of a hipped roof and a chimney stack. The gate was padlocked, and nailed to it was a board which read: *Tregear Estate. Strictly Private. Bawden, Wickett and Lamb, Solicitors, Truro.*

Being house trained and not given to spontaneous acts of van-dalism I decided that I could do nobody any harm by taking a look, so I climbed the gate and dropped down on the other side. As I did so a butcher's van rattled down the lane, but I was in. Rhododendron bushes which had once lined the drive now almost met across it, and under foot there was a thick carpet of rotting leaves. After a short distance the drive forked; one carriageway continued round to the front of the house while the other entered a cobbled stable yard. Green islands of moss submerged the cobbles over a large area, but the buildings were in fair condition though the stable doors sagged on corroded hinges. The back of the house itself, which formed one side of the yard, looked structurally sound though grossly defaced by plumbing innovations undreamed of when the house was built.

It was at this point that I began to feel uneasy, like an intruder—which I was—but my sense of intrusion had nothing to do with the mere act of trespass, it was a more subtle experience as though I had abruptly been made aware that my presence was unwelcome.

The afternoon was sunny and warm, but the yard was in shadow and the stillness was absolute. I walked round to the front of the house where the terrace was beginning to be overgrown by brambles. The terrace was bounded by a stone balustrade with steps which led down to the park and the steps were flanked by a pair of fluted urns. I picked my way across the terrace and stood with my back to the balustrade, looking at the house. It was a gem of its kind, quite unspoiled but somewhat severe; it might have looked more at home in a residential backwater of some cathedral city rather than in this rural setting. The ruby-red bricks were set off by stone coigns; and there were tall sash windows on the ground and first floors with dormers above. The 'shell' canopy was magnificent, the deepest I had seen; worked in a mellow, pinkish stone it rested lightly on superbly carved brackets which seemed to grow out of the pilasters. To my unreasoning disappointment, the ground floor windows were shuttered.

I turned to the gardens which sloped away, largely obedient to the natural contours of the combe. A stream, issuing from somewhere beneath the terrace, followed a winding course across the park and was soon hidden by thickets of camellia and rhododendron. Here and there the sloping sides of the combe had been terraced and planted with shrubs and specimen trees, many of which were exotic and unfamiliar. Above and beyond the furthest trees the sea sparkled in the sunshine.

I went down the steps, past a large ornamental pond in which a life-sized stone nymph rose out of the weed-choked waters, and followed the path by the stream across the park and into the shrubbery. The path through the shrubbery was overgrown and had obviously been much wider, but it was easily passable. Ahead I could hear the sound of a waterfall, and I soon came out on a rocky platform from which the stream dropped twenty or thirty feet in an impressive fall. The platform was overhung by two enormous chestnuts, one on each side of the stream, so that scarcely any vestige of sunshine filtered through their dense canopies. What with the dimness of the light, the roar of the fall and the appearance of total isolation, it was an eerie place and the feeling that I was where I had no right to be returned with greater force. This time I felt a little frightened, but I walked to the edge of the platform and looked down the glen.

In fact, it was a more cheerful and open prospect. The waterfall plunged into a large, dark pool, almost a lake, from which the stream bore away to the left and the floor of the valley broadened, leaving a substantial area of more or less level ground which had been laid out with yew hedges as a maze. At first glimpse I saw the hedges as square and neatly trimmed, defining the complex pattern of the maze as clearly as a geometrical drawing, but it must have been a trick of the light or the working of my imagination, for in fact the hedges were so ragged and overgrown that it was barely possible to make out the line of the paths between them. However, the centre was plain enough, marked by a strange little red-brick building with a steeple like a miniature church, hexagonal in form and ornamented with terra-cotta figures of animals.

The descent was by way of a steep path beside the fall, broken at intervals by stone steps. Though it looked perfectly practicable and I had intended to continue to the cove, I turned back toward the house. To say that I made a dash for it would be an exaggeration, but I admit that I lost no time until I was through the shrubbery and had a clear view of the house. With its shuttered windows it looked blind and desolate in the sunshine.

Once more I was struck by the ineffable stillness. I stood and listened but I could hear nothing, not even the waterfall which could not have been more than three or four hundred yards away.

I walked towards the terrace and there, ahead of me, half-way up the steps, was a girl. She wore a long dress of some striped material and her jet black hair, caught at the neck, hung down her back. We were separated by less than twenty yards and she must have heard me, for she turned to look. She was very pale, with delicate features exquisitely composed, but it was her expression which intrigued and puzzled me. She showed no sign of surprise or concern but neither did she offer any kind of greeting or acknowledgement. She simply turned away again and continued up the steps. At the top she went to the right along the terrace but my view of her was cut off by an island bed of rhododendrons.

Then I realised that there were no rhododendrons, nothing between me and the terrace of which I had a clear view from end to end. Neither was there any girl.

I was deeply disturbed for I was not given to flights of fancy and had never experienced anything of the sort before. I stood for a while staring at the house and trying to recall exactly what it was that I had seen. The rhododendrons had seemed to occupy a considerable area to the right of the pond and they had effectively blocked my view of the eastern end of the house. I felt fairly sure also that I had been dimly aware of sheep grazing near me and of a row of hurdles near the house.

As I drove back to Truro I began to realise what a profound impression the place had made on me; I could not shrug off what had happened. The odd feeling of having been somewhere that was forbidden, the maze which I had seemed to see as it must once have been, and the girl. Girls now dress so unpredictably that it is hardly possible to speak of fashion; to see a girl in a long dress is no more surprising than to see one in trousers or jeans or a mini-skirt. But this girl was different. On reflection, I felt sure that she must have been wearing a half-crinoline or a bustle and she certainly had a distinctive carriage, an easy grace unknown to the modern girl.

I made up my mind then and there that I would see more of Tregear.

At that time I was lodging in a house with two other teachers from the school where I taught: Karen Wilmott, whose subject was English, and Bob Eden, who taught French. The house belonged to a Mrs Rodda ('Call me Clarice'), a widow who was singular in having a liking for schoolteachers and looked after us well. We each had a bedsitter but took our meals together.

Bob and Karen were spending the Easter weekend with their respective parents so Clarice and I were tête-a-tête over our evening meal. I had been at the school only a couple of terms and knew scarcely anybody in the town but Clarice knew everybody. I mentioned the firm of solicitors responsible for Tregear.

'Bawden, Wickett and Lamb—do you know them?'

Clarice was serving the sweet course, a steamed fruit pudding; she liked her food and would listen to no nonsense about slimming. She brushed her red hair clear of her forehead with a plump hand.

'Going to make your will?'

'Something like that.'

'Well, old man Bawden died years ago but Arnold Wickett is still in the business though he must be coming on. Billy Lamb is the same age as me. You mightn't believe it but I might easily have married Billy, we went about together for quite a while.' She passed over my portion of the pudding. 'Help yourself to sauce. Of course, you teach Billy's boy, I've heard you mention him.'

The possible connection had not occurred to me. A boy called Lamb in my sixth form 'set' was one of my most promising pupils and I had met his father at a parents' evening.

'A big chap, red faced, looks as though he's got high blood pressure.'

'That's the whisky.' Clarice sighed. 'You never know how they're going to turn out; it's a lottery.'

'He wasn't my idea of a solicitor.'

'Well, he is one and, according to all accounts, a good one.'

The following morning, Tuesday, I was at the offices of Bawden, Wickett and Lamb in Lemon Street by half-past nine. I was kept waiting only a few minutes. Lamb was in his forties; in manner and physique rather larger than life, but friendly and untroubled by professional constipation.

'Tregear? I don't see why you shouldn't snoop round there if you want to.' He caressed the drooping ends of his bandit moustache. 'The place is a white elephant; God knows what will become of it. Of course the farms are let—no problem there, but the house and gardens . . .' He waved his hands. 'It's all very fine for you conservationists, wanting to save these old places, but who's going to foot the bill?'

'Who owns it? I gather that the old lady was the last of the Bottrells.'

Lamb produced a packet of cigarettes. 'Smoke?'

'I don't, thanks.'

'Neither should I. Bloody silly habit—a form of nipple fixation so they tell me and I wouldn't be surprised . . . Yes, Amelia was the last of 'em. Under her will the estate went to Arthur Clark. The Bottrells and the Clarks have been mixed up ever since old man Joseph Bottrell married Mary Ann Clark way back in the 1840's. Arthur is a very decent sort of chap but he's not interested in the estate. We manage it for him and I expect the rent from the farms comes in useful but he never goes near the place; for that matter he hardly ever comes here. I think I've seen him three times in the seven years since Amelia snuffed it.'

Lamb lit his cigarette and drew on it deeply, letting a trickle of grey smoke escape through his lips and watching it rise.

'Arthur's father made a packet out of property in Canada and Arthur now lives in a little place on the Helford River. He's got no heart or head for business and he spends his time studying bugs.' Lamb sighed. 'Lucky chap! I wish I could, though in my case I think it would be women.' He looked at me with a twinkle. 'Bernard Shaw said that youth is wasted on the young; I think money is wasted on the rich.'

'Do you know anything of the family history?'

'Me?' It was as though I had levelled an accusation. 'Not a thing, there must be plenty of it in our files; we've been looking after the Bottrells since the flood but that sort of thing doesn't grab me, it's all I can do to cope with the here and now.'

The telephone rang and he answered it. 'All right, Celia, I shan't keep him waiting. Mr Kenyon is just leaving. By the way, you might ask Jim to let him have the keys of Tregear—no, not all of 'em, the padlock on the main gate and that little door in the east end . . . Yes, anyway, Jim will know.' He dropped the receiver and looked up with a grin. 'Duty calls.'

I stood up. 'It's very kind of you. When do you want the keys back?'

'I suppose you're on holiday?' Lamb sighed. 'Teachers!—the new privileged class. You might as well hang on to 'em until after the holiday, then you can give 'em to the boy—save you coming in.'

He walked with me into the hall. 'Glad the boy is doing all right, he must have more brains than his father.'

'Just one more question. Is the house still furnished?'

'Good God, no! Empty—stripped. We arranged a sale there within a few weeks of probate. Big affair, made a bomb; some of the stuff had been there since the house was built. The dealers went mad.'

A few minutes later I was out in Lemon Street with the keys of Tregear in my pocket. I bought a packet of sandwiches, a bar of chocolate and a couple of cans of beer, collected the car and set out for St Martin.

The weather was still holding and I decided to try to approach the house from the sea side. My timidity of the day before still rankled and though I now had a key to the main gate I preferred to try my luck from the beach and walk the whole length of the park. I drove to St Martin and turned off down the lane under the elms. Although narrow, the surface was not bad and there were passing places at intervals, suggesting that people must live at the cove or that it was popular with summer tourists, or both. After I had passed the white gate a high stone wall and a screen of trees cut off any possible view into the park and the lane ran more or less straight until it ended in a steep, hairpin bend and I arrived at the cove.

A beach of grey pebbles and coarse sand was backed by a low granite wall. The stream, after passing under the road, ran down the middle of the beach and lost itself in the sea. A grassy area was set aside as a carpark but it was empty except for a tethered donkey cropping the grass. On the other side of the road ten or a dozen cottages backed on the estate. A notice read: *Tregear Estate. Pen-withick Cove is private property and visitors are requested to treat it with respect.*

The cottages were in good repair but they had not been tarted up, and apart from a notice offering ice-cream for sale there was no sign of commercialism. I parked the car at a safe distance from the donkey and walked past the cottages looking for a way in to the estate. Several of the front doors stood open to the road and I could hear a radio playing pop music, but I saw no one. I found what I was looking for at the end of the row, an iron kissing-gate in a high stone wall. But the gate was padlocked and it was impossible to climb over it. I tried my key and found that it fitted; the lock was stiff but the key turned and I was in.

Evidently somebody had, or had assumed, permission to gather fallen timber, for in an open shed near the gate there was a great stack and a sawbench powered by a petrol motor. But there was no-one to be seen. I started to walk up the valley and was soon out of sight of the cottages.

The trees were sufficiently open to allow grass to grow, and there were clumps of primroses, with the promise of a later carpet of bluebells. The slope became steeper so that the stream ran more swiftly between narrow banks, and ahead I could hear the muted sound of the waterfall. Children's voices came echoing down the valley, a boy and a girl who seemed to be calling to each other, though at first I could not make out what they were saying. Then the girl's voice came, shrill and tense:

'Not so high, Charles! Not so high! You'll fall! . . . Gordon, *do* something! *Please*, Charles . . .'

I came out of the trees into the clearing below the waterfall and ahead of me, at some distance, was the vertical wall of rock, at least thirty feet high, over which the stream plunged in a smooth, shining cascade to the pool below. Moss and ferns and even sapling trees had established themselves in pockets and ledges on either side of the fall. To my left a high hedge of yew, ragged and unkempt, was all I could see of the maze.

At first I did not see the children, but when I did I held my breath. There were three of them, two boys and a girl, and they

14

had suspended a double rope from a tree on the very edge of the fall. One of the boys was swinging out over the void, higher and higher; each time he was taken back over the platform he contrived with the skill of an acrobat to impart additional momentum to his next outward swing. I could see the boy's face, set in a trance-like ecstasy. The girl was looking up at him, petrified by fear, unable now even to cry out. I opened my mouth to shout, but I do not know whether any sound came for suddenly the children and the swing had vanished and there was nothing but the waterfall and the trees. I felt as one does on waking from some frightening dream, not sure whether it was a dream and wondering whether I had cried out or not.

Once more I tried to recall in detail exactly what it was that I had seen. The children had seemed to be eight to ten years old; the girl had long black hair, a striking child in a print dress with short sleeves puffed out above the elbows. She had stood, a look of terror on her face, her mouth a little open as though about to scream. The boy at her side—presumably Gordon—was less clear in my mind; I had an impression of a heavily built lad with sandy hair. But it was Charles—the boy on the swing—who remained most vividly in my memory; a slight figure with black hair and a pale face, he wore a white shirt and a waistcoat open down the front, knickerbockers and boots—the boots thrust out wildly into the air as he reached the peak of each swing.

In a daze I climbed the steep path by the waterfall. At one point it skirted a sheer drop to the pool below where the water appeared deep and clear. To the left of the path there was a rocky wall into which a grotto had been cut, a chamber, circular in shape and perhaps ten or twelve feet in diameter. Its walls were covered with shells and in one place certain coloured shells had been arranged to form an inscription: J.B. 1779.

I reached the top and walked back through the shrubbery to the house. I turned right along the terrace to the east end where I had not been before. There was a small yard which communicated with the stable-yard and it was obvious that these were the kitchen quarters. I found the door of which I had a key; it was an ordinary plank door which opened outwards, and I realised that, without giving the matter any thought, I had expected it to do so.

I was in a wing of the house which had been quite invisible from the front. It consisted of several rooms of which I thought I could identify the old still-room, the pantry and the kitchen proper; but in the former still-room there was now a large *Aga* cooker, a massive refrigerator and a sink; presumably things which had not attracted bids at the sale. Paint and plaster flaked from the walls and there was a pervasive sweet smell which was probably due to dry-rot. It was not long before I found my way to the main part of the house through a door covered with green baize, padded and patterned with brass studs. It brought me to the rear of the hall which was lit by a window at the head of the stairs.

I crossed the hall diagonally and entered the drawing-room, where it was just possible to see by the light which came through cracks in the shutters. There was an impressive chimney piece contemporary with the house, the walls were panelled in oak from floor to ceiling with classically inspired dado, frieze and cornice, and the plaster ceiling, decorated with the traditional swags, festoons and floral wreaths, was the equal for craftsmanship of any I had seen. But my enthusiasm for these things had evaporated, they were no longer what attracted me to Tregear.

I wandered from room to room, upstairs and down, and from time to time I stopped to listen, thinking that I had heard movement in the house, but there was nothing, no sound anywhere. I was troubled by things which seem to linger on the fringes of my memory yet would not be recalled. But my attitude had changed, I no longer felt like an intruder, but rather as though I belonged and had rights in the place. I went back to one of the front rooms on the first floor where I had seen a collection of picture frames, a box of books and other items, presumably left over from the sale. Sun streamed into the bare room which was empty except for this pathetic little pile of rejects in the middle of the floor. I sat on the warm floorboards by the window and started to sort them.

Some of the frames still had pictures in them but they were of little interest or value; religious engravings of the *Rock of Ages genre* and coloured prints from calendars. The books were a mixed bag, from *Fire and Sword in the Sudan* to *Grandma's Tales for Little Girls*. Two were school books, a Latin primer and a book of propositions from Euclid; both were inscribed on the fly-leaf in a childish hand: Charles Joseph Bottrell, Tregear 1857. In the box with the books were several old photographs and a number of cuttings from newspapers.

I spread the photographs on the floor and one caught my eye immediately. It showed a black-bearded man seated in a basket chair by the ornamental pond, with the terrace and house in the background. His hands rested on a walking stick and a spaniel dog crouched at his feet; he wore *pince-nez* spectacles which had caught the light, giving his eyes a blind look. He seemed the very epitome of a prosperous Victorian gentleman. Someone had pencilled on the mount: Joseph Henry Bottrell, Tregear. 1862.

The other photographs were all studio portraits and I was about to shuffle them together and return them to the box when something familiar about one of them made me look again. It was a portrait of a girl seated and facing the camera. The sight of the picture gave me a curiously disturbing thrill, for I felt sure that it was the girl on the steps. Her small, exquisitely formed features and her serious, rather sad expression were unmistakable. In the photograph she wore a rather low-cut gown which showed to advantage her long, slender neck and hinted at the gentle contours of her breasts. It was signed and dated: Elizabeth 1868.

The press cuttings were mainly from the *West Briton* and dated from between the wars; they reported events concerned with the estate; garden fêtes, Christmas parties, shows, visits from prominent people—including one from a horticulturally-minded Royal. There was an article from a country glossy on the camellias of Tregear and several from gardening magazines. A folded sheet of newspaper turned out to be another article from a local paper, evidently one of a series. It was dated June 1936.

Notable Cornish Families of the Last Century. Number 5. The Bottrells of Tregear

After referring to the alleged descent of the Bottrells from a fourteenth-century lord of north Cornwall, William de Botreaux, the article went on to describe the expanding fortunes of the family through their mining interests in the eighteenth century and their banking venture in the nineteenth.

The most distinguished member of the family in the nineteenth century was, undoubtedly, Joseph Henry Bottrell, who was born at Tregear on January 21st 1820. Joseph was educated privately and at Oxford, but in 1841, when he had just come of age, his father was killed in a riding accident and he had to take over as head both of the family and of Bottrell, Clyma and Roger's Bank, in which he now had a controlling interest. Eight years later, through the bank, he furnished capital for deepening, extending and modernising the workings at Wheal Mercy near St Day. At the time it was considered a risky, almost foolhardy enterprise and the bank's creditors were understandably critical, but Bottrell kept his head and his credit, and the venture paid so well that in five years the bank had recovered its investment with a handsome profit which laid the foundation for its greater prosperity through the remainder of the century.

In 1844 Joseph married Mary Ann Clark whose family were millers and woolstaplers in Grampound. Unusually for the times they had only three children, the first of whom, a boy, died in infancy of the smallpox. Charles Joseph, their second child, was born in 1848 and his sister, Elizabeth, in 1850.

Joseph had advanced ideas about bringing up and educating his children, being greatly influenced by the writings of Rousseau; in particular by *Emile* which contains the seeds of many modern ideas on so-called progressive education. The children were taught privately, mainly by the curate of St Martin, the Reverend John Bone, a young man of considerable scholarship who later distinguished himself as a missionary in Africa.

On June 20th 1868 Mary Ann died after an illness which had lasted for several years. While still in mourning for her mother, Elizabeth married her first cousin, Gordon Clark, who was employed in her father's bank. There was a greater grief to come. Only five days after the wedding Joseph's twenty-year old son, Charles, died in mysterious circumstances. In a matter of weeks the family had suffered a double bereavement and Joseph had been deprived of a male heir.

In April of the following year Elizabeth gave birth to a daughter, Amelia. Elizabeth and her husband now took the name of Clark-Bottrell and Joseph made it known that his grand-daughter would eventually inherit his wealth. Misfortune continued to dog the family and Elizabeth died at the age of thirty four when Amelia was but fifteen.

When her father married again Amelia remained at Tregear with her grandfather. She never married but concerned herself with the estate which she continues to manage with great success. Joseph died in 1890 and ten years later Amelia sold her interest in the family business to one of the big clearing banks.

Charles, Elizabeth and Gordon—they were all there, and I could still hear the little girl's cry, shrill and tense: 'Not so high, Charles!' and 'Gordon, *do* something!'

I had my lunch sitting on the floor by the window. My head came just above the window sill, so that as I ate I was able to look down into the park, which seemed strangely still and sombre in the afternoon sunshine. I watched, half in fear, half in hope that I might see the children again, but there was no-one and, absurdly, I felt cheated. It was very warm with the sun streaming through the window panes, and it is possible that I fell asleep.

*

' "Unlucky wretch that I am!" ' cried the carter; for he saw that the corn was almost gone.'

The voice, young and clear, was startlingly close. The children were not in the garden but in the room with me—the little girl who had cried out and the dark boy who had been on the swing. And the room was transformed. There was a brightly coloured carpet on the floor and the girl lay on her stomach, her chin

cupped in her hands, looking up at her brother. I had no doubt that
he was her brother, the family resemblance was too strong for it
to be otherwise. The boy sat on a low stool, reading aloud from
Grimms' *Household Tales.*

' "Not wretch enough yet!" said the sparrow. "Thy cruelty shall
cost thee thy life!" and away she flew . . .'

The room was a nursery and the walls were almost covered with
cut-out figures and coloured pictures which had even been stuck
on the door. There was the inevitable rocking-horse, a doll's
house, tops and bows and toy swords and shelves full of well-worn
books. A fire burned in the open grate behind a guard, and
outside it was raining so that the room was dimly lit and the
firelight flickered on the faces of the children.

' "Shall I kill her at once?" "No," cried he, " that is letting her
off too easily; she shall die a much more cruel death; I will *eat*
her." But the sparrow began to flutter about, and stretched out
her neck and cried, "Carter! it shall cost thee thy life yet!" With
that he could wait no longer and he gave his wife the hatchet, and
cried, "Wife, strike at the bird and kill her in my hand." And the
wife struck; but missed her aim and hit her husband on the head
so that he fell down dead, and the sparrow flew away quietly to
her nest.'

The boy looked down at his sister and closed the book. 'That's
the end.'

The girl seemed entranced so that she did not move or speak
and the boy went on: 'It was a silly story; if the old woman had hit
the bird in his hand she would probably have chopped his hand
off anyway.'

'Don't, Charles!'

'Why not? Wouldn't you like to see him with his hand hanging
off and the blood spurting out?'

'Charles!'

Her brother stood up, went to the shelves and returned the book
to its place. I saw for the first time that he had a malformed hand,
the fingers of his left hand were not properly separated and he
seemed to have difficulty in achieving movement beyond his
knuckles. He was small and slender, with black, curly hair like

his sister, a pale complexion and delicate features like the girl's, but in his expression there was a curious intensity which at once marked him off from the generality of children.

'Read me another story, Charles.'

'Read for yourself.'

'But it's not the same.'

The boy came to stand over her and spoke in a lowered tone: 'I shan't read to you any more, ever, unless you come with me climbing tomorrow.'

She raised herself into a sitting position. 'At the cove?'

'That's for babies; I mean the chimney.'

'All right. Is Gordon coming?'

'I suppose so.' The boy grinned. 'He'll probably get stuck half-way up, he's fat enough!'

'Why do you dislike him so, Charles?'

His face clouded. 'I just don't like him.'

The door opened very quietly and a woman stood there, a woman in her late twenties or early thirties. She had probably been an attractive girl but she was putting on weight, her features had an unhealthy puffiness and her eyes seemed unduly prominent. Without the slightest change of expression she glanced round the room, then stood staring at the girl.

'Good afternoon, mamma.'

The woman neither answered nor gave any sign that she had heard.

'Good afternoon, mamma.'

She turned to the boy and a tender smile spread over her features. 'Good afternoon, Charles.'

From the moment the door had opened the children had frozen into attitudes from which they did not relax until it closed again; then the boy turned to his sister.

'You were scared.'

'I *wasn't* scared. Don't be horrid, Charles.' After a little while she added, 'Mamma never speaks to me—never.'

Then, suddenly, they were gone and the room was once more flooded with sunlight though bare and empty. I felt cold and frightened. I got to my feet and went quickly out of the room and down the stairs to the hall. Once I thought I heard laughter but when I stopped to listen there was nothing.

Charles and Elizabeth.

I went through the kitchens and out of the plank door which I locked behind me. I could have walked to the cove to pick up the car by going down the lane, but a streak of obstinacy made me go through the park by the way I had come.

When I reached the rock platform above the waterfall I could hear the sawbench working, and by the open shed near the entrance a man was reducing a stack of boughs to logs. He was elderly but upright and muscular, with surprisingly smooth, brown skin.

"Afternoon.'

'Good afte .noon.'

'You got ousiness in the estate, mister?'

I held up the keys. 'I got these from Mr Lamb, the solicitor.'

'That's all right, then.'

'Do you get much trouble with trespassers?'

'I don't get no trouble with 'em, I just boots 'em out.'

I watched while he sliced up another bough.

'There were children playing above the waterfall this morning.'

He looked at me. 'Children? I ain't seen no children.'

'Three of them, two boys and a girl.'

He shook his head and went on with his work. At the next break I said, 'Did you work on the estate when Miss Amelia was alive?'

'I did, and my father before me and his father before him. My grandfather started work here five or six year before Miss Amelia was born an' she died a few year back at a hundred and one, so you might say we done more than a century between us. O' course, grandfather was here in Mr Joseph's time when things was different. In they days they had a butler, a housekeeper, cook, maids, a coachman an' four or five gardeners.'

'You must know the family history better than most.'

'There ain't that much to know; they was an unlucky family.'

'Joseph's only son died young, didn't he?'

The old man took out his pipe and started to fill it from a leather pouch. 'I don't know about that.'

'In an article I read they said that Charles died five days after his sister's wedding.'

He grinned. 'Well, in that case they must know more about it than I do.' He paused to light his pipe and it was some time before he was ready to continue. 'The fact is, mister, that he *disappeared* five days after his sister's wedding. What happened to 'n nobody ever found out from that day to this and it ain't likely they will now. According to my grandfather he jest walked out of the house that afternoon in the clothes he stood up in and nobody ever set eyes on 'n again.'

'But they must have had some idea, surely?'

'There was plenty of ideas.' He smiled. 'You can imagine in a place like this; people was still talking about it when I can remember. Some said he'd got into a row with a party of gypsies that was in the neighbourhood and that they done 'n in. It seems that he was only a little 'n but strong, and fiery tempered. Others said he must've drowned but if he did they never found the body. Another idea was that he'd just cleared out—got hisself a berth on a ship at Falmouth or jest stowed away.'

'Was there some trouble between him and his family?'

He looked at me with disapproval. 'I never said so, did I?'

I realised that I was not expected to contribute to the discussion and hastened to withdraw. 'No, of course not, it merely occurred to me that if he did leave home of his own accord he must have had a reason.'

'Maybe. As a matter of fact grandfather did tell me that Mr Charles never got on with his brother-in-law, Mr Gordon. They was first cousins and they never got on. Once grandfather catched 'em fighting—that was before the marriage but it jest showed there was no good blood between 'em. Of course, that give rise to other talk.'

'What sort of talk?'

He looked at me with his surprisingly blue eyes. 'Not profitable talk anyways.' He added after a moment, 'Mr Charles had a deformed hand. Grandfather said the fingers on his left hand weren't properly separated.'

I remarked that it was all very sad and he nodded. 'And Miss

Elizabeth didn't make old bones neither, she died in her thirties.'

'She was Amelia's mother, is that right?'

'That's right. An' Amelia lived to be a hundred an' one.' He chuckled. 'Jest as though she was trying to make up for the rest of 'em.'

'Elizabeth and her husband, Gordon, were first cousins, weren't they?' I wanted to keep him going.

'They was. Old Joseph married a Clark from over to Grampound and it was her brother's son as married Miss Elizabeth.'

At that moment I could think of nothing more to ask him but I need not have worried for he went on without any prompting.

'You must've seen the memorial which Joseph put up to his son?'

'No, I don't think so.'

'In the maze, that little brick affair in the middle. Joseph wanted to put up a proper memorial in the churchyard but the vicar wouldn't agree to that because there was no reason to say he was dead for sure. Anyway a year or two after he disappeared his father put up that thing in the maze.'

'How odd! You can't get into the maze now, can you?'

'It's not easy, but that's recent. Right up to within a few days of her dying Miss Amelia would say, "Whatever else you don't do, Blight, keep the hedges of the maze trimmed." An' I did, an' I put fresh flowers on the table in that little building every day or two, just like she used to when she could get about.' He shook his head. 'Now 'tis all gone to pot like everything else and they calls it progress.'

He turned away abruptly. 'Anyway, I got work to do so I'll wish you good-day. Don't bother to lock the gate, I'll be leaving myself in a while.'

I wished him good-bye. 'I shall be coming back most days for the next week or so.'

'Oh, aye. Well, there's plenty of room for the two of us I reckon.'

I arrived back at my lodgings just after four o'clock, when Clarice was giving two of her friends tea. In her forties, Clarice retained enough of her girlish looks to be attractive, though she had put on a lot of weight and was defending her flame-coloured hair with liberal doses of red-rinse.

'One of my clever young people.' That was her standard introduction, but I escaped with one sticky bun and a cup of tea.

'Don't forget, Brian! Dinner at seven sharp.'

Except when Clarice had visitors our evening meal was always known as supper.

CHAPTER TWO

LOOKING BACK, I find it strange that I had so little inclination to seek for any reasoned explanation of my experiences. I was wholly absorbed in the self-imposed task of finding out more about this family with whom I had become so much involved, though I had a curiously persistent notion that through them I should discover something about myself.

On Wednesday morning after breakfast I set out with a packed lunch, my camera, a notebook and a weapon like a billhook which I had spent a long time in sharpening. I parked the car at the cove, which was quite deserted—even the donkey was no longer to be seen—and made for the kissing-gate. Old man Blight must have oiled the padlock, for the key turned easily.

As I entered the park I had an impression of lifelessness. Any naturalist would have been able to show that the woods were full of invisible thrusting life, and in any case there were the trees, shrubs and bracken, the primroses, grass and moss, the lichens and ferns. But despite them all I had a melancholy feeling that life had in some mysterious way come to a halt, its processes suspended.

I made my way upstream to the waterfall, climbed the steep winding path to the rock platform above the fall, and sat where I had a good view of the maze to make a sketch of its lay-out.

Unlike most mazes this one showed no sign of any rule having been observed in its construction; it seemed to have been designed with the sole object of making it as complex as possible and the paths led into each other in a bewildering fashion with very few blank ends. There was no separate exit, so that to get out of the maze it was necessary to retrace one's steps from the centre. It took me about twenty minutes to complete the sketch and once, as I worked, I heard voices not far away, but though I stood up and looked around I could see no-one.

With my completed plan I went down the path and found the entrance. It was not so much overgrown as I had supposed and, cutting and slashing with my billhook, I made steady progress along the paths. Working in this way it took me about forty minutes to reach the centre, and by that time I was hot and tired. Leaves and twigs seemed to have worked their way down inside my shirt, and I was decidedly uncomfortable.

The red-brick building was larger than I had thought. It was hexagonal, with entrances in two of its sides in the form of Gothic arches. The base of the steeple was surrounded by miniature crenellations with a gargoyle-like terracotta animal at each of the six corners. Inside there was a large stone table, also hexagonal, on which an inscription had been carved though it was hardly visible by reason of plaster which had fallen from the ceiling.

I swept the top clean and read: 'The building erected over this table stands to the memory of Charles Joseph Bottrell, who departed from us 25th July 1868 aged 20 years.

'*Speak not evil of the dead, but call them blessed.*'

A strange epitaph, and the phrase 'departed from us' seemed to confirm Blight's version of the story but there could be little doubt that Joseph had believed his son to be dead.

The air in the little building was still and humid and the stone paving felt cold underfoot, but I stayed, thinking that here if anywhere I might expect another of those experiences which step by step, like lessons in a primer, were teaching me more of the lives of those others with whom I had become involved. Nothing happened, and I started back the way I had come. I had gone only a short distance when I fancied that I heard footsteps. I stopped to listen, strangely nervous and tense, but heard nothing. A few more steps and I stopped again, convinced this time that I had been right; there was someone in the maze, someone who moved when I moved and stopped when I stopped. I do not know why I was jittery for it seemed likely that Blight, the former gardener, had noticed that the hedges had been cut back and had come to investigate. The sensible thing was to shout but I could not bring myself to do so.

It is difficult to explain or even to tell of the stages through which I passed from uneasiness to fear and from fear to sheer panic. I referred to my plan of the maze but I was much too confused to make use of it, and I started to hurry down the first path which opened before me. Immediately I was aware of footsteps which seemed to be pacing mine on the other side of the hedge to my right. I stopped and the other stopped also. I tried to peer through the hedge but the growth was too dense and I could see nothing. I broke into a run and took the first left turn which offered, but the footsteps, running now, kept pace with mine. I doubled back, turned corner after corner, now hopelessly lost, but all the time the sound of the other's footsteps kept me company like the echo of my own.

I had an extraordinary fear of coming face to face with whoever it was in the maze with me, but I was still sufficiently rational to be surprised by two things: first, that whichever way I turned the footsteps were on my right and, second, that the hedges on my right were always neatly trimmed and square while those on my left were ragged and unkempt. Even then the idea occurred to me that I was poised on a knife-edge between past and present.

At one point I found myself back in the centre. Suddenly and alarmingly I was out in the open, and like a rabbit I scuttled for the nearest cover so that the absurd though frightening drama was resumed. After a little while I was forced to stop for breath, but when I did the other stopped also. As I stood panting, listening to my racing heart, I was acutely aware of him on the other side of the green hedge, less than a yard away.

It happened that where I had stopped there was a thin place in the hedge and, involuntarily, I stooped to look through. As I parted the few branches I saw him and recognised him at once. It was Charles. His eyes were level with mine and he was staring at me with a slightly mocking smile as though we were engaged in some sort of game in which he was certain of emerging the winner. He was holding back the twigs with his left, malformed hand as I was doing with my right. I glanced down and saw with fascinated horror that my hand was the mirror image of his, that my fingers like his were not separated below the middle joints. Our two hands were almost touching. I saw him look down as I had done and his smile broadened. I had the uneasy feeling that I was looking at my own reflection but that in some way it was the image which had become dominant.

I do not know how long we stood there facing each other, separated by a few straggling twigs, but eventually he turned away and very shortly afterwards I stumbled on the exit.

I was dazed, exhausted and frightened. But it passed. I brushed myself down and began to feel ashamed of the panic which had taken hold of me and to wonder whether I had not imagined the whole thing.

I climbed the path by the waterfall and stood under the trees at the top, looking back at the maze. It was as I had seen it in that brief instant during my first visit. All the hedges were clipped square and the white gravelled paths stood out with geometrical precision. There was no building at the centre, only the hexagonal stone table, and seated at the table in a rustic chair was the boy, Charles. He had two frogs in front of him and he was trying to make them jump over a miniature hurdle made of twigs, but the frogs seemed ready to jump in any direction but the right one and he had some difficulty in preventing them from leaping off the table altogether. Then, suddenly, they were still, squatting, facing each other. Charles whipped out a clasp knife, opened it smartly, despite his malformed hand, and thrust the blade through the body of the frog nearest to him so that the point grated audibly on the stone surface of the table.

'Charles!'

The shout startled me as it echoed round the glen, for it had come from close by. I turned to see a black bearded man standing by me, looking down into the maze.

The boy did not even look up; the second frog had not moved and he had his knife poised to deal with it as he had the first.

'No, Charles!'

This time he turned and looked up at the rock platform. At the distance of the centre of the maze it was impossible to see his

29

expression clearly, but I was struck by the slowness of his move-
ments, almost as though he had been just awakened from sleep. The
second frog had escaped but the first was still writhing on the
stone table.

'Kill it, Charles! Kill it!'

The boy took the heavy clasp knife by the blade and brought the
handle down sharply on the frog's skull, crushing it.

'Now come here, boy.'

The man appeared to be quite unaware of me, though he was
within a few feet of where I stood. I thought I recognized him
as the man in the basket chair in the photograph. He reminded me
of Toulouse-Lautrec, even to the pince-nez, and he wore a broad-
brimmed straw hat not unlike the painter's.

It was some minutes before the boy arrived at the rock platform,
breathing hard from his exertions. He was a good deal older than
when I had seen him in the nursery—twelve or thirteen, perhaps.

'Why did you deliberately injure the frog?'

The boy did not answer and his father repeated the question.

'I want to answer you truthfully, papa.'

'Well?'

'I needed to kill it.'

'But why? Had the creature done you any harm? Did the fact
that it would not jump as you wished anger you?'

'No, papa, it was nothing to do with the frogs not jumping and
I was not angry.'

'Well, then?'

The boy was silent. He seemed neither embarrassed nor resentful
of his father's questions, but unnaturally calm.

'I am waiting, Charles.'

'I need to know, father.'

'To know what?'

'I'm not sure.'

His father was watching him with a worried frown, and when he
spoke his voice was colder, more distant. 'You must try to discover
whatever it is that you wish to know without inflicting suffering
on innocent creatures.'

'Yes, papa.'

'Agreeing with me is not enough, Charles, you must do something about this; this is the third occasion to my knowledge—'

'Yes, papa, I know. I will do as you say.'

His father was far from satisfied with this assurance but seemed at a loss what more to say.

'I wish that you would not spend quite so much time alone, Charles. You should see more of your cousin, Gordon. He does not come here as often as he used to do, and I suspect it is because you have not made him welcome. He is very little older than you but, perhaps, somewhat more mature—more stable '

'Yes, papa.'

The man took a gold hunter from his pocket and flicked it open. 'It is time we returned to the house, they will be holding back luncheon.'

The two of them walked off along the path through the trees and I followed them with my eyes until they were hidden from view. Joseph Bottrell and his son, Charles. From my point of view the most unnerving feature of the exchange between father and son was the fact that I seemed to be aware of what was going on in Charles's mind. I was conscious of the mental turmoil concealed beneath his air of apparent calm and polite attention. The conciliatory words and manner meant nothing; they were no more than a smokescreen to hide mystification, self-disgust and the conviction that he must, in some way, be mentally disturbed. The questions which his father put to him with the concern of a responsible parent he put to himself with an urgency born of nightmarish fear.

Looking back, the ambivalence of my own attitude at that time is shown by the fact that I took my camera and photographed the maze as I then saw it—hedges trimmed and paths freshly gravelled —and I did this so that I might have evidence of the reality of my experience.

It is impossible to describe my feelings as I walked back to the house. I seemed to be in a limbo of existence, aware of two worlds, the one in which I lived my everyday life, and the other in which I was an unacknowledged interloper. My actions seemed to be dictated by some agency outside myself but, strangely, I was not particularly concerned. I accepted my fate with the resignation of a dreamer who knows intuitively that he cannot change the course of his dream.

Once through the trees, I was walking along a well-tended path between shrubs of camellia and azalea. A gardener engaged in dead-heading gave no sign as I passed within a couple of feet of him. The shrubs gave way to open grass where sheep were grazing, and I was in sight of the house. Charles and his father had reached the terrace and were going indoors through the front door which stood open. The east end of the house and terrace were hidden by a great clump of rhododendrons. I crossed the grass, passed the pool where the nymph was deprived of her reflection by a floating carpet of water lilies, and went up the steps to the terrace. I had to move one of the hurdles which had been placed to prevent sheep straying near the house.

Despite the dark panelling, with the front door open and the landing window clean and sparkling the hall was a lighter, more cheerful place. There were portraits of people in eighteenth-century dress, two gilded pier tables with mirrors above, and several chairs. I did not pause in the hall but went straight to the dining-room, to the right of the front door.

There was a long oval table covered with a white embroidered cloth and the table was set for luncheon for five people; three of the places were occupied. Elizabeth was there, sitting primly, her dark eyes staring into space; the woman who had entered the nursery sat at one end of the table, her hands in her lap, her eyes closed. The third person, a woman of about the same age, sat on her right; she was dressed in black satin and wore a widow's cap. The butler stood by the sideboard and on the far side of the room, by another door, a maid waited. None of the five people in the room moved so much as a muscle, and the silence was broken only by the ticking of a black marble mantel clock whose hands pointed to four minutes past twelve.

A small commotion in the hall and Joseph Bottrell came in, closely followed by his son. He stopped by his wife's chair, took out his hunter and checked it against the clock. 'I must apologise, my dear; we were delayed.'

Charles, in his turn, said, 'I apologise for being late, mamma.'

His mother said nothing, she did not even look at her husband, but she turned to her son with a smile which transformed her face. Joseph took his seat at the head of the table and the maid left the room to return a moment later with a tureen which she placed on the sideboard. The five people at the table bowed their heads. 'For these and all thy blessings, Lord . . .'

The butler started to serve.

'Will you take a little wine and water, Mary?'

His wife dropped her spoon and patted her lips with a napkin. 'No.'

'Florence?'

The other woman shook her head. 'Thank you, no, Joseph.'

Joseph turned to the butler. 'The hock, Richards.'

Sun streamed through the high sash windows, gleaming on the porcelain and silver, the linen was crisp and white, the faded Chinese wallpaper with its pattern of cranes and bamboos was still gay, but the atmosphere in the room was oppressive, almost menacing.

Charles looked across at his sister and caught the faintest hint of a smile; she was the only person in the whole world with whom he could make contact. For the rest it was as though he had been caught up in a play in which he had no part.

His father cleared his throat. 'I have to go to London tomorrow on business of the bank. I shall be away three or four days.'

The woman called Florence said, 'I will see that your bag is packed.'

Elizabeth said, 'Shall you cross the new bridge over the Tamar, papa?'

Joseph smiled. 'I certainly hope so, Elizabeth. Unless Mr Brunel has left out a few nuts and bolts so that we fall into the river.'

Elizabeth chuckled and her mother stared.

Florence said, 'The new bridge will be a great convenience to travellers.'

'Yes, indeed. I hope to be in London within ten hours of leaving Truro, whereas in my father's time, indeed in my own youth, it was a journey of four or even five days.'

33

Mary Bottrell, after sipping a little soup, held the heavy silver spoon poised as though uncertain what to do with it, then brought it down with a crash on her plate so that the porcelain was shattered and soup trickled over the tablecloth and dripped to the floor.

The crack seemed to echo in my head like a revolver shot and in an instant they were gone, the dining-room was empty and shuttered, and I was standing in the half-light shivering with shock and fright. I felt a compelling need to be out of the house in the sunshine, so that I almost ran into the hall, through the green door and out through the kitchens.

I was trembling, and I looked round the yard, fearful now that some tell-tale object or scene would mean that I was still in the world of Charles and Elizabeth and their mother, who seemed to be suffering from some disorder of the mind. But in the yard moss covered the cobbles, the doors to the coachhouse hung drunkenly on rusty hinges and the house was as I had first seen it. I walked slowly down the drive to the gate and set off down the lane to the cove where I had left my car.

For the first time I wondered whether I should go on with this strange venture. I was beginning to realise that these experiences had their price, and that this might be higher than at first appeared. It was the way in which I was beginning to identify with Charles that worried me most. I thought of Stevenson's Dr Jekyll. There were parallels, but there were also significant differences. In the beginning Dr Jekyll had deliberately contrived and was able to control his transformations into Mr Hyde, whereas I had never considered the possibility of making excursions into the past and had no idea why they had occurred. As Dr Jekyll lost control the transformation occurred more frequently and lasted longer; something of the sort seemed to be happening to me, but I had by no means reached a point at which my personality seemed to be threatened—though I could see the possibility. Of course I had, or seemed to have, an escape route not open to Jekyll—I could simply stay away from Tregear.

The Jekyll and Hyde story is a parable about our dual natures, about the struggle between good and evil, but here I could see no parallel; in my experiences I had not been able to influence events one way or another, I was simply an unacknowledged spectator. All the same, I had a feeling that I was being confronted with a darker side of my own nature.

As a boy I had passed through a phase in which I had been fascinated by the occult. I had read every book I could get hold of on the subject, fictional and pseudo-scientific. My mother had disapproved. 'What do you want to fill your head with that old rubbish for?' She had shown a similar reaction when in my late teens I started to read psychology. 'It's unhealthy!' I understand her attitude now. There are subjects which it may be dangerous to dwell too much upon.

I arrived at the cove, where my Mini had company in the shape of a Rover 2000 and an elderly couple strolled on the beach, stooping now and then to pick up a shell or an attractive pebble. I had made up my mind. I would not go back to Tregear for twenty-four hours. 'After that, I'll see.' I felt relieved, and drove back to Truro with a sense of having achieved a moral victory, as when I decided to give up smoking.

It was early afternoon and market day, so the pubs were still open and the farmers were having a drink and a chat before returning home. I took my film to a photographer who had a notice outside his shop saying that films left then would be ready by ten in the morning.

'Only about half the film has been exposed but don't worry about that, I want to see what I've taken.'

'You're back early.' Clarice's possessive attitude worried me sometimes. I had an uncomfortable feeling that I filled some particular rôle in her day-dreams, though I could not guess which rôle it was.

'You know that Karen arrived back at lunchtime?'

'I'd forgotten that she was due back today.'

'Oh, yes?' Her manner was arch. 'She's up in her room; the least you can do is to go up and say "hullo".'

'I expect she'll manage without.'

My gruffness, which often amounted to rudeness, seemed to confirm rather than undermine her belief in our special relationship.

I went up to my room and tried to settle down to work on my teaching programme for the next term, but after twenty minutes I gave up, put on a Mahler record and lounged in my armchair with a thriller. My room was at the front of the house, a large room with a marble mantelpiece round the gas fire, an elaborately moulded cornice and a ceiling-rose of plaster grapes and vine leaves. The furniture was well worn but the place had an air of shabby comfort, and I had put up extra shelves for my books, which still overflowed on to the floor.

At five o'clock by the little alarm clock on the mantelpiece there was a knock at the door and Karen Wilmott drifted in. Karen was twenty-three, a willowy blonde, and vague. As usual, she wandered about the room looking at everything before she spoke, and when she did she addressed her remarks to the bookshelves rather than to me.

'Terry is taking Joyce and me to some do at a friend's place this evening and we wondered if you would like to come?'

'Thanks all the same, but I've got some work I'd like to get on with.'

'It's not a party; there's a chap coming who's a hypnotist, a Pakistani or Indian or something. We thought you might be interested.'

'Thanks, but I think I'll give it a miss.'

'It seemed right up your street.'

'Why do you say that?'

'You go to Yoga classes, don't you?'

'What's that got to do with it?'

She shrugged and returned to the bookshelves.

'Don't you like women, Brian?'

'Women? Why shouldn't I like them?'

Her interest shifted from the books to the record player which had just stopped playing. She went over to it. 'Mahler. You like classical music, don't you?'

It was a typical Karenism, something between a question, an accusation and an expression of amused tolerance.

'I like some classical music just as I like some books and some women.'

36

'You're not queer, are you Brian?'

'No.'

'Not that it matters. I quite like queers, they often understand women much better than the other sort.'

'I'm not very well informed on the subject.'

'It's at Feock.'

'What is?'

'This thing—the place where the hypnotist is going to be. I wish you'd come. Terry's getting to be a bore, always fumbling. I think there must be something wrong with him. What's the male equivalent of a nympho?'

'You teach English.'

'Anyway, he's only got one thought in his mind.'

By some obscure process of reasoning it was being borne in upon me that if I did not accept the invitation I should be labelled a queer.

'All right, I'll come if you really want me to.'

Although I have no homosexual inclinations I am not obsessed by girls either, which makes me sensitive to even the softest impeachment.

'You'd better bring a bottle of something—what have you got?'

I went to the cupboard where I kept a small stock of drinks. 'I've got an unopened bottle of Bristol Cream, will that do?'

Karen looked at me in mock amazement. 'Christ! Now we really know how the other half lives. Haven't you got any plonk? Spanish Sauterne? Cat's pee with sugar in it—*vin très ordinaire*.'

'Afraid not.'

'Then it will have to be the sherry, but it had better do for all of us, we don't want to be ostentatious.' She wandered to the door. 'Half seven then. We'd better use your car; Terry's is temperamental.'

Feock is a little place on the Fal south of Truro where yachtsmen congregate; a haven for those who have done well enough out of the rat-race to afford the luxury of being disgusted with it. It is not easy to find by night, and heavy rain which started as we left Truro did not improve our chances. Karen, sitting in the back

37

seat with Terry, issued a stream of confused but peremptory directives, and Joyce—none of Karen's friends have surnames—sitting next to me, talked incessantly. When she ran out of things to say she repeated what she had said before.

We found the place fifteen minutes after the proceedings had been due to start. I had expected to be taken to someone's house but this was a hall which had once been a barn, and there were thirty or forty people milling about chatting, sipping drinks and nibbling biscuits. A cassette player churned out music in which the sitar predominated. I was not introduced to anybody, but a pretty girl in a bib-and-brace overall of plum-coloured velvet took my sherry with one hand and offered me a glass of pale yellow liquid with the other.

'Try our vodka punch, guaranteed to put fur on your tongue.'

I was surprised to see that the average age of the party was probably in the late thirties and I felt happier. Although I am a schoolteacher I am not at home with the young. Somebody appealed to the company to sit down but as there were few chairs most of them had to sit on the floor. Slip-mats had been provided as a defence against splinters from the rough floorboards.

A white-haired gentleman, seated cross-legged on his slip-mat, smiled up at me. 'Are you acquainted with Dr Gupta?'

I said that I was not.

'Then you have a great treat in store; a very great treat. Meeting the doctor changed my life.'

'Indeed.' I tried to sound polite.

'You know him, of course, by reputation?'

I resigned myself to sitting next to the old gentleman and placed my slip-mat next to his.

'Not really. I have heard that he is some kind of hypnotist.'

My neighbour was shocked. 'I assure you that he is a great deal more than that, a very great deal. However, I will leave you to find that out for yourself as so many others have done.'

Karen and the others had deserted me, they were still talking to the girl in the plum-coloured velvet. Somebody offered me a plate of dry biscuits and I took one absentmindedly. There was a

38

minor commotion at the door and an Indian gentleman came in; he was tall, somewhat portly, with aristocratic features and very large eyes. A table and two chairs had been placed at one end of the room and he went over to them. People stopped talking, and those who were still standing found places to sit. The music stopped with the sitar cut off in full cry.

'My name is Gupta, Das Gupta, and I am a doctor of medicine, not a magician or an entertainer.' He spoke in a rather high-pitched voice with a sing-song rhythm which, though monotonous, commanded attention, and as he looked slowly round his audience with those gentle, bovine eyes I began to take him seriously.

'I see here several friends, and others who may become friends before the evening is over.'

I was distracted by Karen who came and sat on the floor by me. I moved up to make room on my mat.

'Sorry,' she said, 'but they've run out of mats.' I wondered what had happened to Terry.

'I have been asked to give a demonstration of hypnotism. It is a technique which I sometimes use in my medical work but, for me, it is much more than a clinical aid; for me it is an extension of the means of communication between one human being and another. In some degree it enables us to transcend the barriers between man and man—that is its chief importance.'

The audience, despite his pedantic manner, was attentive, and it was possible to sense a feeling of expectancy. As he talked the doctor surveyed his listeners, his eyes seemed to rest momentarily on each one in turn, and it was as though a rapport was established through the exchange of a message or signal.

'There are other and more powerful means which may be used to surmount the barriers that separate us one from another and from God, but they require long and strict preparation both psychological and physiological. They do not, therefore, lend themselves to demonstration. If you are content to regard what you see here tonight as a show, then I hope that you will go home having been entertained. There is nothing wrong with that; but I hope that some of you will commit yourselves more deeply and that you may be rewarded by a fleeting glimpse of what I call the *Oneness*

—the unity of life past, present and future, human and divine.'

At first I was acutely aware of Karen beside me, for though her eyes were on the speaker her warm thigh pressed against mine. But as the piping, cultured voice continued I found myself concentrating more and more on the doctor, making an increasing effort to hear and understand. It was oddly difficult, for the Indian seemed to move in and out of my visual focus with disturbing unpredictability, and his voice fluctuated in volume so that some words and phrases boomed in my ears with almost shocking clarity while others faded to a whisper which seemed to come from some far corner of the room.

'You will have noticed that I have spoken of transcending or surmounting barriers, not of destroying them . . . There must be barriers to define the limits of our personality, they are the fences by which we are enclosed. We may properly seek to glimpse what is on the other side of those fences but we destroy them at our peril . . .'

I regained control of my vision and hearing and I even wondered whether I had been affected by the abominable punch. At any rate, I was now able to follow the proceedings normally. Gupta asked for his first volunteer and, out of several, chose a woman in her early thirties, thin and tense. He put her to sit on the chair next to his and held her hand.

'Relax . . . That's right, relax completely, let your body sag, just droop. I want to conduct what is called a regression experiment; to take you back in time through your life and help you to recollect incidents which you think you have forgotten. Are you willing to do that?'

'Yes.'

'Good! Do you mind telling me your age?'

'I am thirty-two.'

'Well, I shall try to take you back through the years, step by step, to the time when you were an infant. You must not be concerned for you will not tell me things you do not want me to know.'

He passed his hands in front of the woman's eyes. 'I am going to put you to sleep. I shall count down from five and when I have finished you will be asleep . . . Five . . . Four . . . Your lids are

40

heavy and you are finding it difficult to keep your eyes open. Don't try; let yourself go . . . Three . . . Two . . .'

That was the last I remembered until I was vaguely aware of Dr Gupta bending over me. The doctor's brown eyes seemed to hover; his head was at a curious angle and I could see the smooth brown jaw, rounded and gleaming faintly with perspiration.

'Are you awake, Mr Bottrell?'

I wondered why the doctor was calling me by that name.

'Yes, of course.'

'Fully awake?'

I realised that I was no longer sitting on the mat by Karen but on a chair, the chair where I had last seen the woman whom Gupta was using as his subject.

'Yes, fully awake.'

'Are you feeling well?'

'Perfectly well, thank you.'

'Better than usual, perhaps?'

'Yes.' It was true. I was puzzled by what had happened but not worried; interested but not concerned. I felt completely relaxed as one sometimes does on waking from a long, dreamless sleep. Even the fact that I must have been the centre of attention for the whole room did not bother me as it would normally have done.

'You must have gone under at the same time as my subject; it sometimes happens to very sensitive subjects. The young lady by your side did not notice for some time, then she thought that you must be asleep. When she could not wake you she became alarmed.'

'I'm sorry, it was foolish of me.'

Dr Gupta was charming. 'My dear friend, do not apologise; you are an excellent deep-trance subject and I hope to have the pleasure of working with you again.'

As I began to realise the implications of what had happened I became increasingly embarrassed. I went back to my place beside Karen. 'I'm sorry that I made such a fool of myself.'

Her voice was warm. 'You didn't, it was very interesting.'

It came back to me suddenly. 'He called me Bottrell.'

The girl chuckled. 'That's what you said you were called. When

41

he asked you your name you said, loud and clear, "Charles Joseph Bottrell".'

I felt cold inside.

'Have you been holding out on us?'

'What? No, of course not!'

'Then why did you tell him you were called Bottrell?'

'I've no idea.'

There were many questions I would have liked to ask her. 'Did I say anything very absurd?'

She squeezed my arm. 'Of course not! Actually he couldn't get much out of you, you weren't on the same wavelength. You said something that sounded like a quotation.'

'What was it?'

'Speak not evil of the dead but call them blessed.'

'God!'

'Anyway, forget it and relax.'

There was a break for more refreshment and Dr Gupta came over to me.

'Have you ever been hypnotised before, Mr Bottrell?'

'No, never.'

'And you have never had any trance-like experience?'

'No.'

He was moving away when I asked him: 'Is self-hypnosis possible?'

He came back and looked at me with greater interest. 'Of course; it usually requires a great deal of self-discipline and practice but it is certainly possible. Many so-called witch doctors depend upon it. Why do you ask?'

'I just wondered.'

He continued to look at me closely. Finally he took out his wallet and handed me a card. 'If at any time you feel that you would like to discuss these things with me I shall be delighted to see you.'

We had two more demonstrations and another short talk and the evening was over. I drove the party home, but this time Karen was beside me and Joyce sat in the back with Terry. We were all very quiet and I supposed that Karen and Terry must have

quarrelled. I dropped Terry and Joyce off at their respective homes
and was left alone with Karen. I felt depressed and vaguely unwell,
as I remembered feeling when I was sickening for influenza.

'Are you all right?'

'Yes, of course.'

'You were looking very pale when we left Feock.'

'I'm fine.'

I parked the car in the drive and we went indoors together.
Outside the door of my room I hesitated, I did not want to face
being alone, but I hesitated too long and the moment passed.

'Good night, then.' She moved off across the landing.

'Karen.'

'Yes?'

'Are you doing anything special tomorrow?'

'Nothing special.'

'Would you like to go out somewhere?'

'Fine.'

'Good! See you at breakfast.'

To my surprise I went to sleep almost as soon as my head
touched the pillow and I did not wake until sunlight was coming
in through the chinks in the curtains. The rain had gone in the
night and it was another fine day.

CHAPTER THREE

KAREN, NEVER AT her best in the mornings, came downstairs in her dressing gown, poured herself a cup of coffee and went back up again without a word spoken. On school days she often left without even a cup of coffee. I had a lightly boiled egg and toast as I have done since childhood. I liked the egg runny enough to dip the toast in the yolk. After breakfast I stood in the front hall, looking down the drive and waiting for the postman; not that I was expecting anything in particular, but I was too moody and restless to sit in my room.

Already I was telling myself that I had been wrong to decide against going to Tregear; if I was going to brood all day, what was the point in staying away? I had committed myself to a day out with Karen, but it hardly looked as though she was enthusiastic. I felt like a reformed alcoholic who talks himself into one little drink.

'Oh, there you are! Ready?'

Incredibly, there was Karen, dressed in slacks and a sheepskin coat, with a bag over her shoulder, looking fresh and cheerful.

I mumbled something about fetching my coat and went upstairs.

In the town, she said: 'If you'll give me five minutes there are one or two things I want to do . . .'

I was lucky in finding a parking space in the main street. Karen got out.

'Boot's and the post office—ten minutes at the outside—okay?'

I was parked within a few yards of the shop where I had taken my film, and it was a quarter to ten. I walked up the narrow alley

44

off the street to the shop. The films had come, but I had to wait for them to be unpacked. In the end I got my little yellow wallet, paid, and returned to the car where Karen was waiting.

'Snaps—may I look?'

The question was a formality; she took the wallet and spread the snaps on her lap.

'Half of them are blank—how's that?'

'The film jammed.' The lie came easily.

They were photographs of buildings I had looked at, mainly churches.

'Are you interested in architecture?'

'Yes, I suppose so.'

'You don't sound very enthusiastic.' She continued to turn over the snaps. 'Hullo, what's this? It's a maze, isn't it?'

I would have hesitated a long time before committing myself to looking, now I had no choice. I saw at once that the maze in the picture was neglected and overgrown. From the snap it was difficult to imagine the neatly trimmed hedges and gravelled paths as I had seen them when I took it.

'Where is it? I've only seen the one at Hampton Court.'

'It's in the garden of a house I went to.'

'Where? Can we go and see it?'

'The gardens are not open to the public.'

'But you went.'

I caught sight of the traffic warden in my mirror and my time was up. I pulled out and joined the stream of traffic going east.

'Where shall we go?'

'To that house, wherever it is. I want to see the maze.'

'But I've told you—.'

'Then we'll gate-crash, it's more fun.'

I did not argue; in the back of my mind I wondered if I had not half contrived the situation.

'Do you know the area round Veryan Bay?'

'I've been to Carhays Castle.'

'It's not far from Carhays; the next cove.'

We stopped at a little shop in Tregony to buy something for lunch. I got some cooked ham and a few bread rolls. Karen pointed

45

to a highly coloured Battenburg sandwich in a plastic wrapping. 'Let's have one of those.'

'Isn't all that marzipan bad for the teeth?'

She laughed. 'I expect so, but let's live dangerously for once.'

Back in the car she was looking at me with a curious expression. 'Is this the sort of thing you usually do when you're off on your own?'

'More or less.'

'You're a strange one.'

For some reason which I cannot explain it had become the proper thing to do to approach the house from the cove, not through the drive gate. I drove to St Martin and turned off down the lane. It was odd having a girl beside me, I kept watching her out of the corner of my eye; her face in repose was serious, withdrawn. In profile I thought that she was almost beautiful.

When we reached the cove she was ecstatic. 'What a place! I'd never imagined . . . It's like going back in time.'

It was high tide and the sea was a level, shimmering plain, stretching away to the horizon and dazzling the eyes.

'It looks good enough for a swim.'

'A bit too early in the year.'

She laughed again. Most things I said seemed to amuse her.

'Who lives in the estate?'

'Nobody, the house is empty.'

'Then there's no reason why we shouldn't have our lunch in the grounds. Let's take the food with us.'

A little boy sat on the doorstep of one of the cottages, playing with a set of wooden bricks, but there was no other sign of life. I hoped that the kissing-gate would be unlocked to avoid unnecessary explanation, but I was disappointed.

'We can't get in!'

I felt in my pocket. 'I've got a key.'

'Well, I'm damned! You don't own the place, by any chance?'

I was embarrassed. 'It's quite simple really. I'm interested in old houses. This one is in the hands of a firm of solicitors and I happen to know one of the partners; he let me have a key to look round '

We passed through the gate and I locked it behind us.

'What a beautiful place! Imagine living here—being brought up in your own countryside!' After a moment she said: 'What's that noise?'

'The waterfall.'

We came out into the open with the waterfall in front of us and the maze to our left.

'It's breath-taking! How long is it since anybody lived here?'

'About seven or eight years. Before that there was an old lady with a couple of servants, she died at a hundred and one. She was born and lived her whole life here.'

'What a wonderful life she must have had!'

This was a new aspect of Karen. I had not imagined that rural life, even in the top bracket, would have appealed to her, but she seemed enchanted. I started to walk towards the waterfall.

'Can't we go into the maze?'

'No.'

Perhaps I sounded brusque, for she looked at me and said quietly; 'Surely there's no reason why we shouldn't look?'

'It's overgrown.'

'All the same . . .'

We reached the entrance, and she saw at once that the hedges had been cut back.

'I'm going in.'

To avoid us both being lost I produced my sketch.

'So you've been in! What's the matter with you, Brian? Have you got the copyright or something?'

As we worked our way through the paths I kept listening for footsteps, but I heard none and we reached the centre. Karen entered the little brick building, saw the table and read the inscription. 'Bottrell—Charles Bottrell . . . and the quotation—"Speak not evil of the dead but call them blessed." It's what you said last night.'

'I know, I've been thinking a lot about this place.'

She made no comment and we left the maze. We scrambled up the steep slope to the rock platform and stopped to admire the grotto and the waterfall. All the time my eyes were alert for any

47

change in our surroundings but everything remained reassuringly normal. We were two people wandering round a neglected estate. As we came in sight of the house Karen stopped.

'It's the sort of place one dreamed about as a child; anything could happen here.'

I was wondering if anything did happen how she would be affected.

The sun was warm, and as we reached the terrace the warmth reflected from the stonework made it seem like high summer. She looked at the shuttered windows and the encroaching brambles.

'What a shame! This place ought to be full of life.'

'Do you want to see the inside of the house?'

Her eyes lit up. 'Could we?'

I led her round the house to my plank door and we went through the kitchens into the dimly lit hall, but the empty, darkened rooms did not impress her.

'They need furniture and people—and, most of all, kids.'

By the time she had seen over the house we decided that it was time to have our lunch, and we sat on the floor in the old nursery as I had done.

'We seem to spend our time sitting on floors.'

She grinned. 'There are worse places.'

While we ate we talked; she told me about her home and her childhood and, to my surprise, I found myself talking too. I told her things I had never imagined that I would tell anyone—not that there was anything strange or wrong about them, just ordinary things, so humdrum and banal that I could not have imagined anyone else being interested.

It occurred to me that she was a very nice girl; that her off-hand manner and her vagueness were a pose. We all put up some sort of smoke-screen. She seemed to me at that moment very pleasant to be with and I was glad of her company.

It was very warm by the window and we were probably drowsy. At any rate I must have closed my eyes, for I opened them to find that the room was a nursery once more, though quite different from how I had first seen it. The rocking-horse and the doll's house were still there, but the other toys had gone, and in place of cut-

48

out pictures stuck to the walls and door there was a flowered wall-paper and white paint. Hanging on the walls were several water-colours in gilt frames. The furniture now included two tables, a couple of armchairs and a painter's easel.

Elizabeth was sitting at one of the tables writing; an older Elizabeth, perhaps fourteen or fifteen. She wore a blue dress with a tight bodice and a full skirt which had inset pleats of a different material with a floral design. Her black hair hung almost to her waist but was caught back from her face by a blue ribbon. She wrote in an exercise book with a steel pen which scratched on the paper and, from time to time, she referred to a book on the table. Occasionally, to free her hands, she placed the pen between her teeth.

It must have been summer, for there was no fire in the grate and window and door were both open so that a slight breeze blew through the room, billowing the curtains and fluttering the pages of her open book. There were footsteps in the corridor and Charles came in. He had grown taller and carried himself with greater assurance; he stood by his sister and the resemblance seemed more striking than ever. He looked down at her work with a slightly patronising air.

'Is that for Jollibones?'

'A Latin precis.'

'Gad! I'm glad I've finished with him!'

'Father says that he is an excellent teacher.'

Charles moved to the window where we were seated and, for an instant, I was sure that there must be actual physical contact, but he stopped within a foot of Karen and stood looking out into the garden. Karen's eyes were closed and she seemed to be asleep.

'Are you happy away at school, Charles?'

He shrugged. 'It's all right. Some of the fellows are very decent.' He held up his deformed hand. 'Do you know what they call me because of this?—The Crab.'

'Charles, is it true that you are sometimes flogged?'

'Of course it's true.'

'But papa chose the school because it is one of the newer establishments, run on more humanitarian lines.'

49

'You will discover, little sister, that even papa does not know everything.'

'Don't be patronising, Charles!'

'In any case, a schoolmaster without a birch is like a squirrel without a tail—liable to fall off his perch.'

After a moment or two of silence, during which she looked fondly at her brother's back, Elizabeth said: 'How do you find mother?'

'How should I find her?'

'Do you not think that she may be a little better?'

'I have told you before that she will never be any better; she will get slowly worse. That is what the specialist from London told father last year. I heard him, I was listening at the door.'

'I know, but—.'

'There are no buts. Our mother is mad, like great uncle Clark and great grandmamma Clark, though great grandmamma is now so old that it makes little difference.'

'But Charles—.'

'What we should ask ourselves is, which of us? You or me?' He turned to face her and saw her startled expression. 'One in each generation, that is how it has been so far.'

'But Charles, the specialist said that mamma's condition was not hereditary and, in any case, there are our Clark cousins.'

'So there are. I suppose we can always hope that it may be one of them. I think that Gordon looks very odd, especially now that he has taken to wearing spectacles.'

'Charles!'

'But father thinks that it will be me.'

'Now you really are talking nonsense, Charles.'

'But it's true. I can tell from the way he looks at me, especially when we are having one of our little talks.'

Charles turned again to the window, and this time he walked straight to it and rested his hands on the sill. It was uncanny, he seemed to be standing where Karen was and I could see them both. Neither looked ghostly or unreal—I cannot explain it.

Elizabeth was watching her brother with an expression of deep concern.

'You are being morbid, Charles.'

50

He did not turn round. 'Very likely; it is one of the early signs; the doctors call it a symptom.'

They were silent for a while, then Charles said: 'Do you see much of Gordon when I am away?'

Elizabeth hesitated. 'Not a great deal. As you know, he is at the grammar school in Truro and he has to stay there during the week, but he is sometimes here at week-ends.'

'Do you go out with him?'

The girl flushed. 'Not often. We have been out riding together, with Priscilla.'

'Do you like him?'

'Charles! Of course I like him, he is our cousin.'

Her brother's face darkened. 'Cousin or no cousin, he is a miserable creeper!'

There was a tap at the door and a plump, pretty maid-servant came in. 'Begging your pardon, Miss Elizabeth, the master wants to see you in the library.'

'Thank you, Kenyon, I shall be down at once.'

Kenyon!—the little rosy-cheeked girl had my name. It was not even a Cornish name!

Elizabeth wiped her pen, placed it in the tray, closed her books and put them away. Charles watched her with an amused expression.

'And why are you called to father's presence, little sister?'

'I think that he wants me to visit Mrs Treloar and the children.'

'Tom Treloar who works for Coleman?'

'Yes. Tom is in the infirmary with a broken leg and the family is in some distress.'

Charles whistled. 'How things have changed! I have been away less than three months, and I return to find little sister taking over the duties of the mistress of the house.'

'You are hateful at times, Charles!'

She went out, closing the door behind her. Charles stood where he was for a moment, then went over to the bookshelves; but instead of taking down a book he knelt on the floor, rolled back the carpet and lifted a section of the flooring. His hand disappeared into the cavity and came out with a leather bag from which he removed a fat manuscript book. He returned the bag to its hiding place and went over to his writing table with the book. For several minutes he sat, turning the pages, then he took up a pen and started to write.

Karen stirred and opened her eyes, but she gave no sign that she saw anything unusual. She yawned and stretched her arms above her head. 'I must have dozed off.'

For me the room seemed to be dissolving in a shimmering haze, outlines became blurred and vanished, colours faded and disappeared. I had a sensation of vertigo and felt cold, so cold that I began to shiver.

'What's the matter, Brian? You look like death.'

I made an effort. 'I'm all right, I came over a bit queer for a moment. It's nothing.'

Once more I had experienced a brief identification with Charles. I had divined his thoughts as though they were my own. In particular I seemed to understand his attitude to his sister. When his feelings were most tender, when he felt that he needed her most, it was then that he was impelled to treat her with cruelty; to fence with her, draw blood, and see the pain and hurt in her eyes. Afterwards he hated and despised himself.

'You are quite sure that you feel all right?'

Karen's persistence made me irritable, and I brushed off her concern.

'What shall we do now?'

'Have you been up into the attics?'

I said that I had not, and we walked down the broad corridor, round the head of the stairs, to a door covered with green baize like the one on the floor below. It opened on to a landing, from which stairs went down to the kitchens and up to the attics where the servants had slept.

Upstairs there was a long passage with four doors opening off on each side. The rooms were all alike in having sloping ceilings and dormer windows. There was a good deal of fallen plaster on the floors and occasional patches of discolouration where the roof had leaked. Apart from a couple of upholstered chairs with their stuffing hanging out the rooms were empty.

'Two to a room, I suppose,' Karen said. 'Apart from the top brass like the housekeeper.'

I was thinking of the girl Elizabeth had called Kenyon. Presumably she had slept in one of these rooms on her truckle bed, with her trunk, a cane-bottomed chair and a half-share in a wash-stand with its ewer and basin.

'My father is a carpenter,' Karen said. 'A century ago I should have had to go into service and been lucky to find a place like this. God! How I would have hated it!'

'It's the other side of the penny.'

'What do you mean?'

'The house, the gardens, the horses on the one side; this on the other.'

I was wondering if there was any way in which I could get back to the nursery and look under the floorboards without Karen. I did not want to risk a need for explanations, and in the end I gave up the idea. All the same, the possibility that Charles's book might still be there excited me.

Looking back, it seems odd that only a few minutes before I had been shivering with cold and shock in the process of returning to normality after one of my experiences. Although each time the recovery seemed to become increasingly distressing, the effects soon wore off and, like certain ailments, were soon forgotten.

We left the house and walked down through the park, past the waterfall and the maze. The late afternoon sunshine filtered through the trees, filling the glen with a dusty, golden light. The old man was there, sawing logs, and he gave us a sardonic greeting.

'Have you decided to buy it?'

'Not definitely.'

He laughed. 'Is this your young woman, then?'

'A friend.'

We let ourselves out by the kissing-gate and walked along past the cottages. Two women were at their doors gossiping, and they stopped just long enough to give us a long, cool stare. We collected the car and drove back to Truro.

It was difficult to realise that, though I had been with Karen all day, she and I had quite different memories to take home with us, and I needed to be cautious; the odd, ill-considered remark could raise questions which I was not prepared to answer. I felt guilty, for it seemed that I was repaying her friendship with deceit, but I could not bring myself to share my experience with anyone.

We were entering the town and a sign over a restaurant prompted me.

'How about having a meal out this evening? There are two or three places, aren't there? We could book a table.'

'Provided we go Dutch.'

'Not on your life! I'm old fashioned.'

She grinned. 'All right, just this once.'

We went back to our lodgings and later, about eight o'clock, we went out to have our meal together. *Potage de lentilles, Coq au Vin* and *Soufflé aux Apricots*. We drank a bottle of wine between us and returned home feeling mellow and with a good conceit of ourselves. For the first time since the previous Monday I had spent three consecutive hours without brooding on Tregear and on the people who lived there.

After that it seemed natural to go to her room, where she made coffee in one of those electrically heated pots which have such a curious repertoire of sounds. The evening had turned cold and we sat in front of her gas fire. Holding hands grew into love-making by degrees, with neither of us forcing the pace. There was no sudden gust of passion but an unhurried advance, like the rising tide. I was entranced by her body, taken unawares by its perfection, and she was sufficiently experienced to guide me in the techniques of love without appearing to do so. Although she was by no means my first girl, my previous love-making had been hasty and furtive; now I had a glimpse of what it might mean to be in love.

It was after one when I left her room and went to my own. My thoughts were confused; so much had happened in a single day. I lay in bed expecting to remain awake for a long time, but I must have been asleep within minutes; then I dreamed.

I was in a bed with side-curtains which were not drawn, so that I was vaguely aware of the room and its furniture, which seemed massive; gleaming in the dim light. I was in bed with a girl; her brown hair was spread on the pillow and she was looking up at me with eyes which were both provocative and a little scared. She had a round, childish face, and her body was so plump that there seemed to be no firmness anywhere. We writhed together, my arms round her, but she would not allow me to part her legs and made little moans of protest whenever I tried to do so.

The extraordinary thing was that I felt no real desire for her, yet I was determined to have her.

'You knew what to expect when you came to bed.'

'But not all the way, Mr Charles. If you do I'll scream.'

'And if you scream, I'll throttle you, make up your mind to that.'

The result was inevitable, her resistance was no more than a charade.

'Mr Charles! You can't, you mustn't! You know what'll happen.'

But her protests subsided and she began to arch her back and twist and turn in a slow rhythm which increased in pace. At last, when I would have separated from her she held me.

'Now, what have you done?'

We lay together, panting; my right hand was still on her shoulder and I saw that the fingers were incompletely separated so that they held her soft flesh like a claw. It was then, in my dream, that I recognized her; she was the servant girl whom Elizabeth had called Kenyon.

I woke in a panic, and however much I tried to persuade myself otherwise I could not escape the conviction that what I had dreamed had really happened, and that it had happened to *me*.

I have no idea how long I lay there arguing in circles, but I reached one conclusion—I would find out whether the girl and I were of the same family, whether, in fact, she was the essential link between me and the Bottrells. As far as I knew the Kenyons had lived for generations in the little Dartmoor village where I was born; my parents still ran the shop which was post-office, newsagency and village store, and my grandparents on my father's side lived a few doors down the same street. It was there that I stood the best chance of finding out what I wanted to know.

I got up early and telephoned my mother to expect me. I did not wait for breakfast, partly because I did not want it but mainly because I could not face Karen. I knew that she would suspect me of running away, or giving our relationship time to cool off. I wished that I could have explained, but that was out of the question.

In the light of day I felt calmer, though no less concerned. I was able to accept that I had dreamed of a relationship with the Kenyon girl, but I had become a dealer in dreams of a sort which were more real than the events of every day. I could not believe in my day-dreams and reject those which came to me by night. It seemed that Charles Bottrell, more than a century ago, had seduced a servant girl called Kenyon; but there was more to it than that. At least twice I had identified myself with Charles, and in this dream I had *become* Charles. I had seen 'my' deformed hand clutching the girl's white body.

Our village is little more than a single street, and a brown Dartmoor stream runs down one side of it. Apart from my parents' shop there is a butcher, a baker, a small garage and a pub. The church is at one end of the village and the chapel at the other. When I arrived my father was out with the van delivering, while my mother served in the shop with the help of a young girl. Every now and then the shop bell jangled and this, with the smell of the place, always brought back more vivid memories than were prompted by what I saw.

Mother insisted on making me a cup of tea and sitting with me while I drank it, though I knew that she was on edge, listening for every sound from the shop.

'What's all this about then, Bri?'

One might have thought that the name Brian was safe from any diminutive, but I have been 'Bri' from the cradle.

'It isn't about anything, I've just come to see you.'

'Oh, yes.'

'I do come home, often.'

She nodded. 'You do, I'll give you that, but not on the spur of the minute, you're not that sort.'

'Well, I have this time.'

'Fair enough and we're glad to see you, but if you're in some sort of trouble I'd rather know about it.'

'Why should you think I'm in trouble?'

'Because you look as though you're not sleeping properly, you look drawn and worried. Is it some girl?'

'There is nothing worrying me.'

She shrugged. 'Oh, well, I'll get back to the shop.'

As I passed through the shop on my way to see my grandparents there she was, serving two customers at once.

'I'm going to see gran, I expect she'll want me to stay to lunch.'

'I expect she will, she usually does.'

It was from my grandfather that I hoped to get the information I wanted. He had memories as well as the time and inclination to recall them. Grandmother was laying places for two on a spotlessly white cloth.

'You know when to come, young Bri, you always did.'

'I haven't come for lunch, gran.'

'No, but you'll stay just the same.' She looked to the kitchen window and to the long, narrow garden behind the house. 'He's about his bits and pieces up in the shed but he'll be down in a minute. What are you doing home, then?'

My grandfather was still an impressive figure, tall and without a trace of surplus flesh. Age had emphasised the sinews of his frame. After asking about my job and my prospects he gave me my chance by talking about Truro as he remembered it from a boyhood visit before the first world war.

'I remember they was building the towers of the cathedral— putting the steeples on—nineteen o' eight or nine, it must 've bin, when I was thirteen or fourteen.'

'Did any of our family ever live in that part of the world?'

He was spearing vegetables with his fork and he looked up at me. 'Funny you should ask that, it was just in my mind. There was a Fanny Kenyon, married a Pascoe from that way; he died young and she went as housekeeper to a family in one of the big houses down there.'

'When was this?'

57

He laughed. 'Before your time and mine too. She was sister to my great grandfather, so work that out!' He paused from eating and considered. 'It must've bin in the fifties or sixties, I reckon—more than a hundred year ago.'

'Can you remember which house it was or the name of the family she worked for?'

'No, I can't, though I must have heard my grandmother speak of 'em often enough.'

'Your grandmother?'

'Aye, she worked for 'em too; when she were a young girl. It was her aunt being housekeeper there as got her the job.'

I must have heard a great deal of talk from time to time about the family history but, like many other young men, I had never been much interested, feeling that I had outgrown my roots. Now I was getting confused.

'You say that your grandmother on your father's side—the Kenyon side of the family—was there in service when she was a young girl?'

The old man looked at me and there was a twinkle in his eye which I did not understand. 'That's right.'

'What was she called?'

'Mary.'

'I mean her surname.'

'Kenyon.'

I suppose that I showed some impatience. 'I mean before she married your grandfather.'

He grinned. 'She never married nobody. Mary got herself pregnant when she was sixteen. O' course she had to leave her place and come home, and my father was born here in the village. He were a bastard and he took his mother's name.'

Granny was annoyed. 'You've no call to talk that way.'

The old man was laughing. 'They call it illegitimate these days. We still don't talk about it though God knows why, with all that goes on.'

'So you don't know who your grandfather was?'

'No, she never would let on; not even when she was an old woman; but it were somebody rich, for they give her six hundred pound, and that were a lot o' money when a man was getting twelve and sixpence a week and you could buy a cottage like this for forty pound.'

'And your father's Christian name was Charles, wasn't it?'

'What's that got to do with it?'

'Nothing—nothing. I was trying to get it straight.' I wondered what he would have said if I had told him what was really in my mind—how vividly I had dreamed of the moment of conception of his father.

'Did you know her well—your granny, I mean?'

'Of course. She lived to be eighty something. I mind that she died on my birthday—I must've bin thirty-five or thereabouts.'

'Thirty-six.' Granny took a hand. 'It was January nineteen thirty one and the churchyard was under a foot of snow when they buried her.'

'What was she like?'

Grandfather frowned. 'People liked her well enough; she was always active, busy about the place.'

'Interfering,' Granny said.

'I meant, what did she look like?'

'A little thing, no more than up to my chest.'

'But fat,' Granny added, 'as big round as she was long.'

The old man nodded. 'True enough in later years; even when I first remember her she was on the plump side.'

Granny said: 'There's a photo of her in the sideboard drawer in the parlour. You can see it when you've had your afters.'

We ate baked rice pudding with a delicious brown skin on the top and drank two cups of strong tea each before I was allowed to see the photograph. It was a postcard-sized studio portrait, faded and sepia coloured. It showed an elderly woman seated in a basket chair; she was very fat, with heavy features, so that she reminded me of Queen Victoria in her later years.

'That's like she was—to the life.'

It was an uncanny sensation. This was the fresh-faced girl who had come to the nursery with a message for Elizabeth from her father, and this was the girl I had seduced in my dream.

If I had interpreted the facts correctly she and Charles Bottrell were my great-great-grandparents. At least I had found out what I had come for.

I stayed the night with my parents and drove back the next day. It rained steadily, but there was little traffic on the road and I had time to think.

I realised that I was becoming obsessed by the Bottrells; I was reaching a point where I could think of little else. If I told anyone of what had happened to me in the past few days I should be looked upon as mentally deranged, yet I had come to accept these experiences as almost normal. That was one of the most disturbing features of the business, I was not sufficiently worried about what was happening to me. Is it not characteristic of certain forms of mental illness that the patient insists on his normality?

And the frequency and duration of these experiences was increasing, suggesting a pattern of addiction. What was more, they were beginning to encroach on my dreams. I found that particularly significant, for while I could stay away from Tregear I had no control over my dreams.

The previous night, in the bed I had slept in as a boy, I had dreamt again of Mary Kenyon—not a coherent narrative dream like the first, but a series of glimpses, like clips from a film. I saw her about her duties at Tregear, sweeping and polishing, making herself unobtrusive. I saw her in the drawing-room, tending the fire and tidying the grate. I saw her in the stable yard, hurrying away, red-faced, from an encounter with the stable boy, and finally I saw her in 'my' bedroom, making the bed, the black material of her dress stretched tightly over her buttocks.

I arrived back at my digs in time for lunch. Karen was there but so was Bob Eden, who had returned the evening before. Bob was a year younger than I, plump, sandy haired, with blue eyes that were magnified by the thick lenses of his spectacles. He was a friendly chap and, sensing that there was some strain between Karen and me, he made conversation. I said scarcely anything, and from time to time I caught Karen watching me. I ate little and left the table early, having made up my mind what I would do.

As I came downstairs with my mackintosh on my arm, Karen was in the hall.

'Are you all right, Brian?'

'Of course.'

'You don't look it.'

'Just a family upset.' I tried to put warmth into my voice, 'Nothing to do with us.'

CHAPTER FOUR

I TELEPHONED FROM a public call-box and remembered, only just in time, that Dr Gupta had addressed me as 'Mr Bottrell'.

'Dr Gupta's secretary speaking.' A thin, girlish voice.

'My name is Bottrell—Charles Bottrell . . .' It gave me a curious feeling to tell this simple lie. 'I met Dr Gupta at a demonstration which he gave recently in Feock, and he suggested that I might telephone him.'

She went away to enquire, and a minute or two later I was speaking to the doctor himself.

'Mr Bottrell? . . . Yes, I remember you perfectly. I hoped that you might telephone. You wish to see me?'

I said that I did.

'Is it urgent?'

I was excited, and I think that my voice must have trembled 'It seems so to me now.'

'Ah! If you will wait for one moment, please.'

There was a brief pause, then he was back. 'Could you come at five o'clock? . . . Splendid! You know where I live? . . . Good! . . . I shall look forward to seeing you.'

Gupta lived in a large Victorian house on the outskirts of the city. It was a gloomy place, with a short drive bordered by laurel bushes leading to the front door. The house was built of grey stone with granite coigns, and there were large bay windows upstairs and down. The doctor answered the door himself.

'Come in, Mr Bottrell, let me take your coat . . .'

I was shown into a room at the back of the house which was furnished as a consulting room; it looked out on a garden with trees, but the lower panes of the window were obscured. I could hear children playing outside.

We sat in black leather armchairs with no desk or table between us.

'I must tell you first that my name is not Bottrell but Kenyon.'

He looked at me with interest but said nothing.

'Apparently I gave you that name under hypnosis—Charles Bottrell—but my real name is Brian Kenyon.'

'Have you any idea why you did not give me your real name?'

I had started with a certain amount of bravado to compensate for my nervousness, but already I was beginning to relax. The room seemed to be restful, and the doctor's steady gaze was in no way embarrassing but rather reassuring.

'Yes, I have, but it's all part of what I want to tell you. The trouble is that my story is so bizarre . . .'

He smiled. 'I am a doctor, Mr Kenyon, and I think I can say that after thirty years of study and practice I am unlikely to be surprised by anything. Neither will you find me unsympathetic.'

I began haltingly. Describing how I had first visited Tregear only five days before was like trying to recall events of childhood.

'It is difficult to believe that so much has happened to me in so short a time.'

'Time is relative, Mr Kenyon. We measure it more realistically by the succession of our own experiences than by the clock or calendar.'

When he interrupted or prompted me it was usually with some such platitude, but his words were always oddly reassuring, and it was not long before I was telling my story with a freedom and lack of self-consciousness which I would not have believed possible. He was a good listener.

When I had finished he was silent for a while, then he said, 'You recall the so-called regression experiments I conducted at Feock?'

'Yes, they were remarkable.'

'Such things are often done but they do not work with everybody; the hypnotist needs a good subject, for success depends as much on the subject as on the hypnotist. From your response on

Wednesday evening it is evident that you must be an excellent deep-trance subject.'

'So?'

Gupta smiled. I think he was pleased that we were now on a conversational basis, that I was no longer responding as to an interrogation.

'Have you heard of the Bloxham tapes?'

'I don't think so.'

'A man by the name of Bloxham carried out a large number of regression experiments with deep-trance subjects, and it seems that he was successful in securing recall, not only of experiences in childhood and infancy, but of incidents in other lives which seemed to have been lived by his subjects.'

'Other lives?'

He looked at me with his large, mild eyes. 'Yes, other lives, Mr Kenyon. You of all people should not be in too much hurry to reject the possibility.' His manner was almost waggish. 'At any rate it seems that a number of people, under hypnosis, were able to give coherent accounts of experiences which they are supposed to have had in a previous existence. In several instances the accounts included information—topographical detail, technical items and little-known but recorded historical incidents—which could be, and, to some extent were, verified. This was possible because what the subjects said while in trance was recorded on tape.'

The doctor sighed. 'It is not for me to pass judgement on the reports of such experiments; until they are repeated under strictly controlled conditions, and with a larger number of people, one must keep an open mind. But from what you have told me it seems that you are making an identification with another life without the assistance of a hypnotist.'

'And you believe that to be possible?'

The doctor spread his plump hands. 'How can I know? You are in a better position to answer your questions than I am.' He must have seen the look of disappointment on my face, for he added at once: 'Don't mistake me, Mr Kenyon, I think you have come to me for help and I will try to help you, but I should be doing you no service by pretending to be more credulous than I am.'

'I understand that, but I would like to persist in my question. Are you prepared to regard it as possible that I am able to recall and seem to re-live incidents from a previous life?'

He thought for some time before answering, then he looked at me solemnly. 'Yes, I am willing to consider such a thing as possible, provided there is a genetic connection between you and the person whose experiences you recall—in other words, provided you are a descendant of that person. From what you have told me it seems that you may be.' He got up and walked to the window, where he stood, looking out over the frosted glass to the garden where children were playing. After a moment he turned to face me once more. 'I am not a mystic or an astrologer or a *guru* or any of those things which Europeans associate with people of my race. I am a medical practitioner and I believe in the methods of science. Having said that I am still willing to look at alleged phenomena which are not explicable in the light of present knowledge, convinced that if they are genuine phenomena they will ultimately be explained. For example, hypnosis is a well-established technique but we do not understand it, it cannot yet be fully explained in scientific terms. One day it will be.'

His objective approach and his readiness to talk were exactly what I needed. I realised that they were of more real comfort than what I had hoped for—a kind of blanket reassurance, a meta-phorical shoulder to weep on.

'I expect you know something of Gregor Mendel and his discovery of the laws which govern inheritance in almost all living things.'

'A little.'

'Well, in the middle of the last century, when Mendel did his research and formulated his laws he had no idea that he was giving a statistical description of the transcription of what we now call the genetic code, a process which goes on at the molecular level in every living cell. I suppose that it is just possible that our inheritance includes another code—a "clan code" which transmits some sort of memory from an individual to his offspring.' He laughed. 'But if you have any molecular biologists among your friends I shouldn't canvas the idea.'

'It would need to be a very elaborate system to provide the detail which I seem to remember.'

Gupta pursed his lips and frowned. 'Perhaps, but it is notoriously difficult to distinguish between what one actually remembers of a given incident and what is supplied out of the general store of one's knowledge. More often than not we embroider our memories, quite unconsciously.'

He came back to sit in his chair and looked at me with a half smile. 'I am a doctor and you are not my patient so I must be careful to avoid anything which might be interpreted as treatment. All the same I am going to ask you if you would like to try a regression experiment of the kind carried out by Bloxham. It certainly will not do you any good, it may not even work, but if it does the results could be interesting.'

I did not hesitate for long. 'Yes, I should like to try it.'

I was put to lie on a couch and he produced a small, portable cassette recorder. He placed the microphone on a table not far from my head.

'Now I shall hypnotise you and try to take you back through your life to infancy and beyond. I shall ask you questions and, of course, my questions and your answers will be recorded. This will be unlike the experiences you have told me about, for it is probable that you will remember nothing of what happens to you between going to sleep and waking again.'

He drew the curtains across the window so that the room was very dimly lit.

'Try to relax—let yourself go. Imagine that you are without bones or muscles and that your body sags on the couch. Look at me. I shall count backwards from seven and before I reach one you will be deeply asleep . . . Now close your eyes . . . Seven . . . Six . . . Five . . . You are falling asleep, you cannot help yourself . . . Your eyes are shut and you are too tired to open them . . . Four . . .'

And that was all I remembered. The next thing I knew I was looking up at him feeling slightly bewildered.

'Didn't it work?'

He smiled. 'Oh, yes. I think it worked very well; you were asleep for twenty-three minutes. How do you feel?'

'All right—fine.'

'Fully awake?'

'Oh, yes.'

'Then if you will go back to your chair we will listen to the recording.'

Dr Gupta's secretary has since made a copy of the tape with a transcription and I have the transcription with me as I write, but I have listened to the tape so often that I could recite it from memory and I know its every scratch and crackle. After asking me various questions which involved memories of my life at different ages, questions and answers of no interest to anyone but me, he came to the real point:

'Now we have arrived at the time of your birth. You were born on February 20th 1953. I am going to take you back through the years before that date, and from time to time I shall ask you if you have anything to tell me. I shall count down from five and when I have done so we shall be in the year 1900—fifty-three years before your birth as Brian Kenyon. Do not tense yourself. Total relaxation, every muscle relaxed. I shall start counting now: Five . . . Four . . . Three . . . Two . . . One . . . We are now in the year 1900, have you any memories of that year?'

There was no response, I could hear on the tape only what I took to be the sound of my breathing, deep and regular.

Dr Gupta resumed: 'Now I am taking you back another twenty years. You are still completely relaxed and deeply asleep. Five . . . Four . . .'

Once more he counted down and put the question, 'Have you any memories of the year 1880?' Again without result. He repeated the formula for each of the years 1870 and 1869 . . . 'Have you nothing to tell me?' And then, 'Does the name Charles Bottrell mean anything to you?'

When I listened to the tape for the first time it was at this point that I realised I had not told him the year of Charles's death.

'Five . . . Four . . .' He counted down again. 'We are now in the year 1868—'

He broke off, seemingly startled by the most extraordinary sound I have ever heard from a human being. Listening to the tape I found it impossible to believe that it was I who had made it. There was stertorous breathing accompanied by a sort of whinnying sound and broken now and then by a hideous gurgling.

Gupta's voice came smooth and calm. 'You are distressed; calm yourself. Breathe more deeply and slowly . . . Calm . . . Deeply asleep. Is it that the year 1868 distresses you?'

The answer came in a barely audible whisper, 'Yes.'

'Very well, let us go further back, perhaps to a time that has pleasanter memories for you.' He repeated the count down. 'Now it is 1861—the year 1861. What is your name?'

'My name is Charles Joseph Bottrell.'

I could scarcely recognize the voice as my own, it sounded so young and boyish, and there was certainly more than a hint of the Cornish brogue.

'How old are you?'

'I am thirteen years old.'

'When were you born?'

'I was born on April 29th 1848.'

'It is now April 29th 1861 and the time is evening. What day is it?'

'It is my birthday.'

'Yes, your thirteenth birthday. What day of the week is it?'

'It is Monday.'

There were considerable intervals between question and answer, and words seemed to come slowly both to the doctor and the subject with whom I still find it difficult to identify myself.

'Have you had an enjoyable birthday?'

There was some hesitation and a false start. 'Yes . . . yes, but papa is angry with me.'

'Why?'

'Because this afternoon I went over to Hemmick to see them killing pigs.'

'Were you interested in seeing the pigs killed?'

68

'Yes. They hang them up by the legs, then they cut their throats and drain off all the blood. The pigs make a dreadful squealing noise.'

'Your father disapproves of you going?'

'He is very angry, he says that I am cruel and insensitive.'

'And what do you say?'

'I'm not sure.'

'Did you enjoy seeing the pigs killed?'

'I am glad that I saw it.'

'Do you enjoy inflicting pain or seeing pain inflicted?'

There was a considerable pause and it seemed that there would be no answer, but Gupta made no attempt to hurry the boy and the answer came at last:

'Yes, I think I do, but at the same time I am sorry.'

'Sorry for the victim?'

'Yes.'

'Why?'

Another long pause. 'It is the same when I suffer pain, I am both glad and sorry at the same time, I cannot explain it.'

'Are you being punished for going to Hemmick this afternoon?'

'Yes, I have to stay in the house all day to-morrow.'

'Have you had some birthday presents?'

'Yes. Papa and mamma gave me a watch and a book called *The Year Book of Facts*: it is all about science. Aunt Florence gave me a prayer-book with gilt edges to the leaves and Elizabeth gave me a book of Lord Byron's poems which she bought with her own money.'

'Do you like Lord Byron's poems?'

'Yes. He is my favourite. Elizabeth likes Tennyson.'

'Where are you now?'

'In our day-room that used to be our nursery, with Elizabeth.'

'Describe the room to me, please.'

'It is just an ordinary room with chairs and cupboards and shelves for our books and there are two tables, one for Elizabeth and one for me.'

'What is your sister doing now?'

'She is writing, doing some exercises for Jollibones.'

'Who is Jollibones?'

There was a faint chuckle. 'That is what we call the curate; his real name is the Reverend John Bone, but he looks so dismal and he speaks with such a solemn voice that we call him Jollibones.'

'Is he your tutor?'

'He used to be, but now I go away to school and he only teaches Elizabeth. Papa says that Mr Sandfield, the vicar, doesn't pay him much and he is glad of the extra money. Papa says that he is a very good teacher.'

'Where are the others?—the other members of your family?'

'Papa and mamma are in the drawing-room because aunt Florence has gone to visit her friend at Philleigh.'

'Why do you say that your father and mother are in the drawing-room *because* your aunt has gone to visit her friend?'

'If aunt were at home, papa would be working in the library but mamma must not be left alone.'

'Why not?'

'Because she tried to kill herself by taking laudanum.'

That was the end of the tape. After we had finished listening to the play-back Dr Gupta switched off the machine and turned to me. 'It is very strange; I have come across nothing like it in my experience, and there can be no doubt that you are involved in some great adventure of the mind.'

'Do you think that the experiences I have had are real? Or do you think that I am suffering from hallucinations?'

His brown eyes rested on me and it was obvious that he was considering very carefully what he would say. 'I do not think that I can answer your question in that form. If you are asking me whether, in my opinion, you are mentally ill, my answer is certainly not. You are venturing into virtually unexplained territory where there are few if any landmarks to guide you.' He smiled. 'An explorer is necessarily a lonely person, forced to rely on what inner resources he can muster, for there is nobody he can look to for help. Most of us are constantly looking over our shoulders to make sure that we are not too far out of step with our neighbours, but the explorer, the innovator and the creative artist have nowhere to look; like Gulliver they must create their own standards. Needless to say, that kind of loneliness demands a great deal of courage.'

'Are you advising me to go on?'

He looked at me oddly. 'Are you sure that you have a choice?'

We talked for more than an hour and he made me promise to come again whenever I felt the need to discuss what was happening to me. It was evening, and dark when he came to the door with me and stood watching me as I walked down the drive. My visit had achieved the very opposite of what I had hoped for; instead of a recipe for escape I was presented with a challenge.

'You must try to recover your original attitude of mind, when you still saw yourself as conducting an investigation into a unique and intriguing experience. If you see yourself as a victim you will certainly become one.'

I walked down Lemon Street to the town centre. There was a fine mist, scarcely to be called rain, and there were few people about; shops and offices were closed, and I was faced with the prospect of returning for my evening meal to be eaten under the eyes of Clarice and Karen, both of whom were beginning to treat me like a rather obstinate child who is sickening for an illness but will not admit it.

My session with Dr Gupta had made it clear to me that even had I wanted to there was no way in which I could withdraw from my involvement with Tregear and the Bottrells. I had committed myself too far or, perhaps, I had never had an option. In any case, I saw the wisdom of Gupta's advice. If I had to recall or re-live further episodes in the life of my *alter ego* it was better that I should do so in a spirit of enquiry and adventure rather than be coerced in fear and reluctance.

It was as I was crossing Boscawen Street that the change took place; the lights suddenly dimmed and for an instant I thought that there had been a power failure. Then I realised that what light there was came from gas lamps with flickering bat's-wing burners which did no more than create a small island of light round each lamp post. I turned up King Street, past a row of small shops, each with its gas jet or oil lamp burning inside. My surprise had been confined to that instant of transition, after that the surroundings had no interest, they were too familiar.

A scurry of rain sweeps down the street and it is bitterly cold. I turn up the collar of my ulster and hurry into High Cross where my father's carriage is waiting outside the bank. Parsons, our coachman-groom, is attending to the carriage lamps.

'Good evening, sir.'

'Good evening, Parsons. Is my father not out yet?'

'No, sir. Mr Clyma left ten minutes gone so I don't suppose the master will be long now.'

I push open the oaken door which has screwed to it a shield with the monogram BCR, done in brass. Bottrell, Clyma and Rogers. A similar shield is fitted to the bars in front of each of the bank's windows and the same monogram appears on the firm's stationery. There are no customers but two clerks are entering up their ledgers. In the next room Roskruge, the senior clerk, is writing letters with a quill pen, having no use for those 'newfangled steel things'. Roskruge has been with the firm forty years; he started in 1821, 'the year the Emperor died' as he is fond of saying—meaning, of course, Napoleon.

'Good evening, Mr Charles.'

'Good evening, Roskruge. Is my father alone?'

'He is, sir; Mr Clyma left a few minutes ago and Mr Rogers— well you know Mr Rogers, sir, he never stays long.'

My father attends the bank on four days a week and usually he leaves at three, but once a month there is a meeting of partners and such meetings often last into the evening. On ordinary days he rides from Tregear on horseback, but in bad weather or when he expects to be late returning he will either use the carriage or stay at Danzig House, our little town house in Quay Street which is looked after by a married couple.

I go through into my father's office, where he is engaged in putting various documents into the huge green safe which is built into the wall to the right of the fireplace.

'Ah, Charles, I am almost ready.'

My father has very white and even teeth which seem all the

more conspicuous in contrast with his black beard, and from infancy I have always been a little frightened when he smiles.

'Did you have a pleasant day with your friends?'

I have spent the day with the Rowse family at Tregarthen. Tom Rowse is a schoolfellow of mine, and at the beginning and end of each term we travel to and from school together, but we have little else in common. However, it is considered necessary that we shall exchange one visit during the holidays. Tom has three sisters but I find them poor company. Tom has scarcely an idea in his head beyond ball games and his sisters are plain and sanctimonious.

'Yes, papa, it was enjoyable.'

'Good! You should see more of those young people, you need more companionship when you are home from school. You and Elizabeth depend too much on each other.' He stands with the safe key in his hand. 'Look, my boy, each of those bags is full of sovereigns.'

'Yes, papa.'

'Of course it is not the money that matters—the money is merely a symbol of our customers' trust, of the faith which they have in our bank and in my conduct of its affairs. It is that faith, Charles, which makes me proud to be a banker.' He closes the big door and turns the key. 'Can you understand that?'

'I think so, papa.'

'And shall you feel the same?'

'I cannot tell how I shall feel.'

'But you wish to join me in the bank when the time comes?'

'It seems the sensible thing to do, papa.'

As always, my lukewarm attitude disappoints him. 'Have you ever thought of other employment?'

'No, papa.'

It is true. When I think of the future it is not of being a banker, a lawyer, a churchman or whatever else a young man of my station might become; my view of the future is vague and troubled. It seems to me that I am caught up in a stream of events which must lead, eventually, to some great climax, but I cannot guess when that climax will come or what its nature will be. I am not frightened of the prospect, but I have this conviction of impotence which makes planning and speculation a waste of time.

I follow my father through the two outer offices. 'Good night, Roskruge! Goodnight, Tippett . . . Rosewarne . . .' And outside, in the windy, rainy darkness, 'Well, Parsons, here we are.'

Why do I marvel at these routines which make up the pattern of my father's life? I have no idea, but I would feel no less of a stranger at the court of the Czar.

We sit back on the cushions and my father spreads a rug over us; the carriage pulls away and rattles down King Street.

'Do you get on well with your cousin Gordon?'

'Well enough, papa.'

'I suppose you realise that the Clarks are not comfortably situated?'

It is an understatement. Uncle Arthur has a milling business in Grampound which is heavily mortgaged, and more than once he has been saved from bankruptcy only by help from my father.

'As you know, although Gordon is just seventeen, a few months older than you, he is already at work in his father's business.'

I wonder what is coming. Am I to be taken into the bank at once instead of going to Oxford?

'He seems to be a very capable young man, but I do not think that his prospects are very good in his present employment, and I propose, with his father's approval, offering him a post in the bank. Our business is growing and we need someone with the right background to train as a future manager. Roskruge is loyal and competent but he is getting old and, in any case, his ideas are outmoded.'

I should be flattered by these confidences but they mean nothing to me.

'I am telling you these things because from now on I want you to know what is in my mind concerning the bank. You see the wisdom of this?'

'I think so, papa.'

After a brief silence he goes on, 'A week from today we shall be celebrating Christmas with the usual family party. I propose to broach the subject to your uncle then. If you see Gordon

74

in the meantime you will say nothing to him of the proposal.'

Because of the wind and the rain the journey is taking longer than usual, and while we are still climbing the hill through Tregony father examines his watch in the light of the carriage lamp. 'We are already late for dinner.'

Through the little front window I can see water cascading off Parsons' oilskin cape. Apart from the carriage lamps there is not a glimmer of light anywhere. The mean little houses we pass seem to be in total darkness.

I sense that my father has more to say to me but I cannot guess whether I am to be rebuked, exhorted or informed. He is clearly ill at ease.

'It is less than three months since that disgraceful affair with the Kenyon girl. You were punished, the girl was adequately compensated and I agreed not to refer to the matter again. Indeed, I forbade any reference to it in my hearing.'

'Yes, papa.'

He snaps. 'Surely it is time you stopped addressing me as "papa" —"father" would be more appropriate.'

'Yes, father.'

'However, what I wish to say is that I am not unaware of the temptations which beset a young man. You should strive to resist them; to find active, healthy employments which divert the mind.'

'Yes, father.'

'Do not resort to self-gratification if you can avoid it. It is a bad habit.'

'Yes, father.'

Another silence, and this time I am sure that he has said all that he intends, but I am wrong.

'In Truro there are one or two houses where men meet girls for a certain purpose. You should know that there are great and terrible risks in such encounters. For one who frequents such places there is a virtual certainty of disease. You understand me?'

'Yes, father.'

'Avoid them at all cost. On the other hand, if you have, on occasion, a compelling need, you can with some confidence visit a house in Goodwives Lane, run by a Mrs Kilthorpe; she is discreet and her girls are . . . her girls are clean and in every way satisfactory.'

I am speechless.

He adds after a moment. 'But I will have no more scandalous conduct with the servants, you understand?'

'Yes, father.'

He tries to relax the tension. 'Aunt Florence will be wondering what has become of us!'

We reach the ford at Hick's Mill where the level of the water is as high as I have ever seen it and the carriage is pushed sideways by the strength of the current.

My father sighs. 'Another mile and we shall be home.'

Aunt Florence is waiting for us in the hall. 'I heard the carriage. What unpleasant weather!'

Greetings exchanged, my father kisses her lightly on the cheek and enquires: 'And Mary? How has she been today?'

Aunt Florence, as always, adopts an offensively oily manner when speaking of my mother and refers to her as 'we'. 'We are not at all well today. We have taken one of Dr Jordan's little pills and we are having a sleep.'

My father sighs. 'I do not know what I should do without you, Florence.'

I go upstairs to our day-room and aunt Florence's voice, now dry and brittle, follows me: 'Dinner in fifteen minutes, Charles!'

Elizabeth is sitting on the rug in front of the fire, reading, her usually pale face slightly flushed by the warmth.

My father is a good man; my mother is insane. These are facts but they mean almost nothing to me. Elizabeth is my sister and I love her. How often in the course of each single day do I think these quite pointless thoughts which lead to no conclusion?

It is very strange that the time occupied by these excursions into the past seems to bear no relation to present time. This episode began while I was crossing Boscawen Street and when it was over I had reached my lodgings. I experienced all the distressing recovery symptoms to which I was becoming accustomed and I hung about outside the house until I was sufficiently composed to face Clarice

76

and the others. I realized that I had broken new ground, for this was the first time I had re-lived any part of Charles's life which had taken him outside Tregear. It was also the first time that I had so completely identified with him as to be totally unaware of my own existence. In this experience I had been in no sense a spectator.

When I eventually went indoors Clarice was on the point of serving the meal.

'Oh, there you are! I was wondering about you. If you like to go up and wash your hands it will be on the table.'

We ate together, Clarice, Karen, Bob Eden and I. Once more the conversation was stilted, with long difficult gaps. Afterwards I went up to my room and a few minutes later there was a tap on the door and Karen came in. She behaved as always, ignoring me at first, making her customary tour of inspection, then she spoke while still turning the pages of one of my books.

'It's that place, isn't it, Brian?'

'What place?'

'Tregear.'

'I don't know what you are talking about.'

Her blue eyes were watching me with a concern which should have flattered but merely embarrassed me.

'Come off it, Brian! That business with Dr Gupta, then our day at Tregear. How did it go? "Speak not evil of the dead but call them blessed." You quoted that and gave your name as Charles Bottrell under hypnosis. Are you in trouble? You look ill. If you go back to school on Tuesday looking like that they'll send you home again.'

'I have no intention of going back to school on Tuesday.'

She looked startled. 'Have you told Mason?'

Mason was the headmaster.

'No.'

'Don't you think you should?'

'I suppose so.' I was indifferent. School and everything else which had dominated my life and thoughts until a week ago were no longer of any importance.

'What's all this in aid of, Brian?'

At the moment I was on the point of telling her the whole story as I had told it to Dr Gupta, but something stopped me. If I had done so the subsequent course of events might have been different. As it was I repeated in a colourless voice: 'I have no idea what you are talking about.'

I saw her expression harden and a little later she left.

I had decided that it should be possible to discover whether I had truly re-lived episodes from another incarnation or merely suffered the most vivid hallucinations. After Karen had gone I spent some time trying to recall the details of what had happened to me in the past week, and I had to admit that I had seen and heard little which could not have been conjured out of my own knowledge and imagination, without the need to invoke a supernatural agency or a theory of regression.

I made this admission to myself with reluctance because hallucinations are a form of mental illness. At any rate, it seemed important to try to settle the question. To do so it was necessary to identify scenes or events of which I had no prior knowledge but which subsequently proved to have been recorded or could in some other way be shown to have happened. For example, in the unlikely event of my finding Charles's manuscript book under a loose floorboard in the old nursery, I should have good evidence that I had indeed re-lived those moments of the past when, after his sister had been called away by the maid Kenyon, he had taken the book from its hiding place.

I had already 'seen' a good deal of Tregear as it supposedly was in the mid-nineteenth century and I had come to 'know' the people who lived there; surely by looking up the family records I should be able to check the accuracy of my observations, enough to decide between recollection and hallucination. So far I had had no contact with the present owner of Tregear, Arthur Clark, but it seemed now that I should get very little further without his help or, at least, his tacit approval. I decided that I would go and see him, but before I did so I would pay one more visit to Tregear.

CHAPTER FIVE

ON SUNDAY MORNINGS Clarice stayed in bed until nine o'clock and neither Karen nor Bob Eden was likely to be seen before ten or eleven. I got up early and made myself some coffee, and by half-past eight I was driving through the deserted streets of the town on my way to Tregear. I reached Tregony without seeing a soul, and I could not help recalling the journey I had made over the same ground in my 'other' life. Then the carriage had rocked, not only because it was buffeted by the wind but also because of the ruts. Now there were no ruts but the weather was much the same, with a gale out of the south-west, and several times the Mini slewed to the left, blown by the force of the wind. Down the valley at Hick's Mill there is now a bridge, but brown water swept along beneath it, and it was not difficult to imagine the horses having to plough through, with the carriage being tugged sideways by the strength of the current.

As I entered St Martin I seemed to have a momentary glimpse of the green with ancient elms, the mounting block outside the inn and the old vicarage with its walls buried beneath a rampant growth of ivy. But now there was no green, only a small car-park, no elms and no mounting block, and the vicarage stood empty, falling into ruin.

It would have been foolish to have gone to the cove and had to walk up through the estate in the rain, so I unlocked the white gate and drove into the stable yard. One of the drains must have been choked, for part of the yard lay under several inches of water.

It was difficult to believe that I had held the keys for only five days, that six days ago I had never heard of the Bottrells of

Tregear; now it was unthinkable that I should return to school on Tuesday and hand over those keys; that I should no longer have the right to enter the house or even to walk in the park.

I let myself into the kitchen area through the plank door and, owing to the rain, the old place seemed more than usually damp and dark and the atmosphere of mouldering decay depressed me. I passed through the hall and upstairs to the nursery where the tall, south-facing window let in all the light there was, making the room relatively more cheerful. I had an unreasoning hope that I might find Charles's book in his secret cache under the floorboards.

I went to the bookshelves in the alcove to the right of the fireplace and knelt where I had seen him kneel. At first I could see no sign of a loose floorboard, but then I noticed a thin joint less than a foot from the skirting; I inserted my nails and lifted. The board came up quite easily, leaving a cavity about eight inches wide and ten in length, a dark little hole in which I could see nothing. I put my hand in and groped about, gingerly at first, then with my whole arm reaching as far as I could. I could feel the plaster-lath work of the ceiling below and I could feel the joists on each side but that was all, no leather bag and no book.

I stood up, disappointed, brushing the dust and cobwebs from my sleeve. I was in a curious mood, not only waiting for something to happen and assuming that it would, but irritated by the delay. I felt that I had committed myself afresh to this strange business and that I had a right to expect results. It was nonsensical, but that was my mood. However, time went by and nothing happened.

I went into the corridor and tramped from room to room; I stood by the windows of the front rooms, looking down at the dripping park. I was working myself up into a state of petulance like a child deprived of a promised treat. I looked at my watch; I had been in the house an hour.

I tried downstairs, in the drawing-room, the dining-room, the library, even in the kitchen, but the rooms remained obstinately silent and dim. I do not know how many times I went up and down stairs, I even visited the attics, for I had a vague idea that it might be necessary for me to be in a certain place at a certain time for the transition to occur.

For the first time I realised how helpless I was to prompt or encourage any happening; I knew nothing of the circumstances which might contribute to an experience, and I had not bothered to try to analyse what had happened on previous occasions. With a sense of real shock it dawned on me that I might never undergo another transition; the bizarre flash-backs might have come to an end as inexplicably as they had begun. The thought filled me with dismay and with something very like panic.

Then, suddenly, all was well. There was carpet under my feet and the air was warm instead of damp and chill. I was standing in the corridor outside the nursery. Waxed woodwork of doors and wainscot gleamed in the subdued light from the landing window; the walls above the wainscot were hung with red flock wallpaper, and there were paintings in heavy, gilded frames. A huge *jardinière* stood on the landing opposite a long-case clock whose hands showed a quarter past two. I could hear its sonorous tick in the otherwise silent house.

Standing there I felt acutely nervous and exposed, so that I looked at each closed door with apprehension and it came home to me how much an interloper I was in this house of a century ago. But after a little while my fears passed; I remembered that I had stood in the dining-room while the family were at luncheon, that twice I had been in the nursery when Charles and Elizabeth were there and once Karen had been with me. So it was unlikely that I need worry about any encounter I might have. All the same I continued down the corridor with great caution, and as I reached the head of the stairs I was touched by a feeling of ineffable loneliness.

Seen from the top of the stairs the hall was transformed; there were framed portraits on the walls and a pair of carved and gilded pier tables with mirrors above faced each other across a large Persian carpet whose rich colours seemed to glow. There were upholstered chairs and, suspended above the stairs, a great wrought-iron lantern of Moorish design. I stood and listened, but apart from the ticking of the clock the house was wrapt in warm, opulent silence.

Unaware of any intention I seemed to be carried along by a will other than my own, and when I reached the bottom of the stairs I crossed the hall to the drawing-room as a matter of course. As I reached the door I heard someone playing the piano, and I opened the door on a familiar scene which aroused not a flicker of interest.

My mother is at the piano. In her periods of normality she plays the piano often; she is said to be an accomplished performer and her doctors admit that it is better for her than any treatment they can prescribe. My aunt Florence is seated on a low chair by the window, working at her embroidery, and she looks up at me with one of her slow, sarcastic smiles which seems to say: 'I know, my boy! There is nothing you can hide from me.' In the years since she came to live with us I have grown to hate her. I leave the room, closing the door behind me, and I go through the hall and out into the stable yard. I am in one of my black moods.

All day I have known that this might happen; that at some critical moment, taken off guard, a look, a word, would penetrate my defences and I would be possessed of that irrational, smouldering fury which sometimes takes hold of me. It springs from an intolerable inner tension which seems to be partly physical; my throat feels constricted, I experience a dull ache at the base of my skull and over my eyes; my teeth clench and all the muscles of my body become taut. I find it easier to ward off such attacks when Elizabeth is with me, it is as though through her I acquire an extra skin, an outer defence. But she has gone to the Rogerses who are giving a party for their pudding-faced daughter, Marion.

In the yard the September sunshine is warm and Wilkes, the stable boy, is grooming Liza, my father's Cleveland bay which he uses for riding.

'Saddle Liza for me.'

He is a tall, gawky boy of my own age, very fair, almost white; slow and stupid and obstinate. He stands looking at me for some time, then he says, 'I can't do that, Mr Charles.'

'Why not?'

'You do knaw why not, Mr Charles; your feyther said not. I'll saddle the pony for 'ee.'

'Damn the pony! Where's Parsons?' Parsons, our coachman-groom, is in Truro with my father, as I well know.

'He's not 'ere, Mr Charles.'

He turns away to resume his grooming of the mare, but I catch him by the shoulder and swing him round. I put my face close to his: 'When my father is away you take orders from me.'

I can see the golden fuzz on his chin and smell his sweat. I wonder what the outcome will be; if I hit him will he fight back? Will he dare?

Gordon comes into the yard, peering at us short-sightedly through his spectacles.

'Oh, there you are, Charles. I thought of going for a swim, would you care to come?'

To be truthful, I am not sorry to be extricated from the absurd position I am in. I let Wilkes go and he returns to the mare as though nothing has happened.

'All right, if you like.'

Gordon wants my company as little as I want his, but he thinks that by making himself agreeable to me he will please my father, his 'rich uncle'.

Our Clark cousins live in a converted farmhouse between St Martin and Grampound. Gordon is the eldest and he has a brother, John, and a sister, Priscilla. Priscilla is the same age as Elizabeth. They live precariously on the income from my uncle Arthur's wool and milling business with occasional help from my father.

Gordon is now working in the bank and, according to father, he works very hard and shows a great aptitude for the business. He is more than a head taller than I and heavily built. I am repelled by his ungainly lumpishness, his ridiculous glasses and, most of all, his scheming; one feels that his every action is carefully considered in relation to what he is pleased to call his 'prospects'.

We walk down through the park in silence until we reach the cove which is deserted except for Molly Couch, who is sitting on a stool outside her cottage, nursing her baby. The baby's fat, pink fingers clutch at her white breast.

'Good afternoon, Molly.'

'Good afternoon, gentlemen.'

Molly has gypsy blood, black hair and eyes and a wild look. Although she married Billy Couch a year ago she is still barely seventeen.

'I suppose you know that anybody can have Molly when Billy is out with the boats?'

This is not true but I say it to excite Gordon, and he flushes as I knew he would.

'She doesn't wear drawers so all you have to do is to back her against the kitchen table and pull up her skirts.'

He says nothing for he cannot trust himself to speak.

'Have you ever had a woman, Gordon?'

He does not answer.

'You should try Molly; she'll surprise you. She's a pretty girl and her belly and thighs are as white as her breasts.'

I am torturing him. I hold up my clawed hand. 'She likes this, the sight and feel of it excite her.'

The images I am implanting in his mind will trouble him for nights to come. Why do I do it? It brings me nothing but self-disgust.

We climb over the rocks to a tiny cove where we undress, and I am amused to see that, although he is anything but shy of his pink, podgy body, he keeps his back to me.

I swim out, leaving him in the shallow water, but not too far out because the current is strong at this tide. I lie on my back and float. Above me puffs of white cloud seem to drift in an abyss of blue so that I feel giddy, but the venom that is in me seeps slowly away. It is at such times that I come nearest to making peace with myself. I think of the mysterious future which has both stimulated and threatened me since childhood. I see it as a great climax, and beyond it—nothing. Is it the family taint of madness which will possess me?

I return to the beach and find Gordon already dressed. We walk back to the cove and turn into the park. He seems thoughtful and we do not exchange half-a-dozen words, but as we draw level with the maze he says:

'Charles . . .'

I assume that he wants to talk about Molly Couch but I am wrong.

'You must promise to keep this to yourself, Charles.'

I am amused. 'I promise.'

'Does Elizabeth ever speak of me?'

'Elizabeth? Of course she speaks of you, what do you think she does—use the deaf-and-dumb language?'

'I mean, does she ever speak of me in a kindly way?'

'I haven't noticed; she doesn't speak of you unkindly—why?'

Gordon puts on his best banker's manner, solemn and judicial. 'In two years Elizabeth will be eighteen and I shall be twenty. At eighteen girls often start thinking about marriage . . .' He is looking at me with his small, shrewd eyes but I still do not grasp what he is getting at.

'Marriage?'

'Yes, Charles. I know that we are both very young to be thinking about such a thing but time slips by . . . I would be prepared to wait indefinitely, but I would like to have some idea of Elizabeth's feelings toward me. I mean, if she definitely dislikes me it is useless for me to continue to think of it.' He pauses, then adds, 'It may seem strange to you, Charles, but I like to look ahead, to know where I am going . . .'

I can scarcely credit my ears. 'You are talking about marriage to Elizabeth?'

'At some time in the future—yes. Your father thinks that I shall do very well in the bank and if Elizabeth is disposed to think kindly of me . . .'

In other circumstances I might have found the situation amusing, but this afternoon, with what has gone before fresh in my mind, I am contemptuous and outraged by his effrontery.

He is looking at me solemnly through his steel-rimmed spectacles and there are little beads of perspiration under his eyes. 'I hope that I am not offending you, Charles?'

Perhaps he has seen my expression.

There are two things which contribute to the violence of my response. One is the very feasibility of the idea—it could happen. I can see him doing so well in the bank and ingratiating himself with my father to the point where father begins to look on him as a suitable son-in-law. As for Elizabeth, unless she changes, she might well do as her dear papa wishes.

At the same time I can see Gordon's naked body, pink and ungainly, as he turns away to hide the fact that my talk of Molly Couch has excited him. I have a momentary vision of him with my slim, supple, exquisite Elizabeth, and I see him through a red curtain of fury.

He is staring at me, evidently startled, and I lash out, catching him with the back of my hand across his cheek, the whole weight of my body behind the blow. His look of astonishment is ludicrous; he makes no attempt at retaliation and does not even raise his hand to his reddening cheek.

He says: 'You should not have done that, Charles; there was no call for it. I offered no disrespect to Elizabeth, on the contrary—'

'Shut up and fight.'

'I see nothing to fight about.'

'What's the matter with you? Are you a coward as well as a creeping sneak?'

'I am not afraid to fight, Charles.'

'Then get on with it.'

He has gone very pale except for the marks of my hand on his cheek. 'If that is what you want . . .'

He is wearing a jacket and waistcoat and the very deliberate way in which he takes them off and hangs them from a branch increases my fury. His spectacles are placed carefully in the pocket of his jacket. I am wearing only a waistcoat and I tear it off.

'Is it to be wrestling or fists?'

'Fists.'

'If your father hears of this I hope that he will not think it was I who—'

'To hell with my father!'

We move to a cleared area where the ground is soft after rain and he frames up but makes no move to come at me, so I hit out with my right and he parries easily; he deals me a moderate blow on my left shoulder. I try again with a similar result, this time his fist glances off my left arm. After a minute or two I realise that he is playing with me, that if he wants to he can make every punch tell; his reach makes it impossible for me to close with him. In a blind rage I rush at him like a mad man and succeed in landing a punch to his throat. It is a painful blow and his expression changes. He replies with a heavy punch to my nose which spurts blood, and immediately he jumps back and drops his guard.

'This is ridiculous, Charles. There is nothing for us to fight about and if your father . . . Let's drop it.'

He takes my agreement for granted, otherwise he would be better prepared. I rush at him and leap on him, my arms round his neck and my legs twined round his thick body. He staggers about for what seems an age, then falls backwards with me on top of him. I get to my knees and start to rain blows on his unprotected face. My fury has now broken loose and is totally beyond my control; it no longer bears any relationship to either cause or justification, and I would certainly kill him if I knew how.

It surprises me that he makes so little resistance; his podgy features are stained with blood which drips from my nostrils and his eyes are half-closed with the whites showing. It dawns on me that he must have hit his head on a root in falling, but the knowledge makes no difference and I continue to belabour him.

I am aware of vague shouts and suddenly I am lifted bodily off him, my arms gripped from behind.

It is Harry Blight, one of our gardeners, a powerful fellow with shoulders like hams and a grip like a vice.

'What's all this, Mr Charles? Do you want to kill him?'

It is an extraordinary sensation and truly frightening; one moment I am twisting round to look up into Harry's bearded face, acutely aware of his painful grip on my biceps, the next I was a spectator, standing apart, watching Charles Bottrell being restrained in the grip of this giant while Gordon lay prone on the ground, his face covered with blood. But my arms ached, my nose and lips felt bruised, and my knuckles smarted as though they had been skinned. I was trembling violently, my heart raced so that it seemed impossible that it would ever recover its normal rhythm, and I was gasping for breath.

I do not know how long I remained there, propped against a tree. I must have closed my eyes for a time, for when I opened them I was alone, it was raining hard and there was no evidence of the fight. It must have been raining for a long time for the trees provided no shelter and water ran from my hair, trickling over my face. My jacket and trousers were soaked through.

I seemed to have been drained of every scrap of energy but I made my way slowly back to the house and went indoors. For a time I stood in the dimly lit kitchen shivering, but whether this was from cold or shock I do not know. I ached all over as though I had been in a real fight, but I could see no sign of injury anywhere.

One of the oddest features of the experience was my knowledge of Charles's reaction. Even as I watched him being hauled off Gordon I had been keenly aware of his dawning realisation that he had come close to murder; and I knew that blended with his relief was the chilling fear that next time help might not arrive until too late.

The shivering was getting worse and I realised that I must get warm or risk being ill. There was plenty of paper and firewood about the place, so I decided to light a fire in the nursery grate. I laid the fire and set a match to it, and after two or three preliminary puffs into the room it drew well and soon I had a roaring fire. I hoped that no one would see the smoke and come to investigate.

When the room began to feel warm I undressed and draped my trousers and jacket over an empty packing case to dry. I found part of a block of chocolate in one of my pockets and when I had eaten that I felt better.

I am well aware that the much abused word, schizophrenic, does not mean split personality in the sense in which it is commonly interpreted, but in that sense—the idea of a dual nature—it exactly describes my situation. I was beginning to feel torn apart by opposing claims on my individuality and I remembered Gupta's words: 'I speak of transcending or surmounting barriers, not of destroying them . . . these barriers define the limits of our individuality, they are the necessary fences by which we are enclosed . . . We may properly seek to glimpse what is on the other side but we destroy them at our peril . . .'

Had I, unwittingly, destroyed such a barrier?

CHAPTER SIX

PROBABLY BECAUSE I had now decided on a definite plan I slept better than I had done for several nights, and woke feeling relaxed and composed. When I had washed and dressed I packed my largest hold-all with things I would be likely to need for an absence of a week or ten days, and by the time I had done this I could hear Karen moving about in the next room. As an afterthought I put in my little transistor radio. I timed it so that I arrived at breakfast just after her.

Clarice greeted me with the kind of sad smile one reserves for invalids 'You've had a bit of a lie-in this morning, it will do you good.'

Karen was eating her cornflakes and saying nothing. I took the plunge. 'I'm afraid I've been more than a bit tiresome recently. You are both perfectly right, I'm not well and I've decided to go home for a few days. I shall telephone the school and tell them not to expect me for the first fortnight of term.'

Karen looked up. 'Have you seen a doctor?'

'Yes.'

'The county will want a certificate.'

I'm not a good liar and it was obvious that neither of the women believed me, but they could hardly say so outright.

Clarice said, 'I'll give you a hand with your packing.'

'I've already packed.' I added, 'Don't let my room.'

'As if I would!'

Karen walked out with me to the car. 'You haven't telephoned Mason.'

'No, I'll do it from a call-box.'

She stood at the gate and watched me drive off down the road.

I felt guilty. But I did stop at the nearest call-box to ring the headmaster. Mason answered, smooth and cautious as always. 'Oh, Brian! What can I do for you, my dear chap?'

'I'm not well, I seem to have some sort of breakdown . . .'

'Indeed? I am sorry.' His tone had become rather more frosty. 'Does that mean that we shan't see you tomorrow?'

'I'm afraid that it does. I'm going home for a few days. I'm sorry, I know that it will be a nuisance at the beginning of term.'

'You've seen a doctor?'

'Oh, yes.'

'And he has advised you to take some time off?'

'You'll be getting a certificate.'

'My dear fellow! That's the least of our worries; it's you I'm concerned about . . .'

'Yes, well, thank you.' I rang off. Whatever they might have been in the past and whatever they might be in the future, Mason, school and my classes meant nothing to me then.

While I was in the call-box I made a second call, this time to Arthur Clark at Helford.

He answered the telephone himself, a cultured Lord-David-Cecil type of voice. He listened to my somewhat confused account of what I wanted. I told him that I was collecting material for a history of prominent Cornish families and that I was particularly interested in the Bottrells.

'Do you want to come and see me?'

'Yes, if that is convenient.'

'Then come, dear boy . . . When? Whenever you wish . . . This morning, by all means.'

Lamb, the solicitor, had said that he was a pleasant chap and he certainly sounded friendly. It was a classic April day with watery sunshine and very occasional showers. There is a pedestrian ferry from Helford Passage to Helford village so, instead of driving round the head of the river, I left my car and took the ferry.

The little village fringes a creek and consists of no more than fifty houses. There were several boats moored off and others were stranded on the shingle for it was low tide. Slow moving men in polo-necked jerseys were working on some of them. They told me in the pub that Clark lived on the other side of the creek. There was a plank bridge across, high enough to clear the spring tides, but now it spanned a few yards of muddy gravel and an anaemic stream. Most of the houses were no more than cottages but they had large gardens which looked almost tropical with echiums, door-mat palms and yuccas mixed in with the azaleas and camellias. Clark's cottage was on a ridge with a steeply sloping garden.

I was struck by the name on the gate, *The Harmas,* and, uncharacteristically quick-witted, I recalled that it was the name Henry Fabre, the insect man, had given to his wilderness garden. I pushed open the gate and was immediately confronted by Clark himself. He was standing just inside the gate smoking a pipe with a long, slender stem. He was a big man, heavily built, but though his features were fleshy he had an air of refinement. He wore a nondescript sweater with holed elbows and a dirty pair of khaki drill slacks. When he looked at me his eyes wrinkled into a squint as though he had difficulty in focusing. His welcome was casual and friendly.

He waved a hand in a gesture which took in the weedy garden with its long grass, nettle patches, docks and sapling trees. 'You see, I am no gardener.'

'Never mind, the name of the place gives you a respectable alibi.'

He grinned and seemed pleased. 'When I was a boy, Fabre was my idol. Perhaps he still is.'

He led me up a steep winding path to the cottage, past a greenhouse full of potted plants and insect cages of fine net. The door of the cottage stood open into a room which occupied the whole ground floor and evidently served as living-room, library, laboratory and study. There was a musty smell, not unpleasant, and everything in the room—books, furniture, rugs, walls, pictures and ceiling—seemed to have acquired a common patina, no doubt compounded of smoky emanations from the open fire and from his pipe.

He cleared a pile of books from a chair which had broken springs. 'There you are, sit you down.'

He continued to stand, a bulky silhouette against the light.

'You are interested in the Bottrells?'

'And in Tregear, it's a grand old house.'

'Yes, but, like many pleasant things these days, it's a liability.'

'You have never thought of living there?'

He shook his head and glanced round at the over-crowded room. 'I like everything within arm's reach; in any case, it would cost a fortune to run.'

We talked about the fate of country houses and the people who had owned them. 'Our society is in a late stage of metamorphosis and God alone knows what will hatch out.' He tried out his epigram with a mischievous grin.

'I suppose you knew Tregear when Miss Amelia was alive?'

He nodded. 'Although my parents settled in Canada I went to school and to university in England and most of my vacations were spent at Tregear. In so far as anybody can be held responsible for my upbringing, I suppose it is Amelia. She was already in her sixties when I was at prep school, but she had the vigour and drive of a young woman.'

We talked for a while of life at Tregear and of his relations with Amelia, which seemed to have been warmly affectionate on both sides.

'She was a remarkable woman. She taught me about plants and animals—not only in the formal, biological sense, but in a way which made me feel that we and they are on the same footing in the world.' He smiled. 'As though we had equal rights.' He added after a moment: 'Amelia had a profound respect for life and some of it rubbed off on me.'

It was pleasant to sit there with the door open to his wilderness garden with the sun streaming in, and I felt envious; this man was living a life which I often imagined for myself—a selfish life, I suppose, surrounded only by those things which bore the imprint of his own personality.

His pipe had gone out and he re-lit it, perching himself on the edge of a table where there were a binocular microscope, a lamp and several small glass dishes.

'She should have married and had children of her own; I have often wondered why she didn't, but I think there was a shadow over her youth.'

I said nothing, and after a little while he went on, evidently not sorry to have someone to talk to. 'There was insanity in the family on the Clark's side, and Amelia's mother, who died when Amelia was fifteen, had married her maternal first cousin. There are letters to Amelia from a friend which refer to her fear of the "family taint".' He smiled and looked surprisingly youthful.

'Although she was such a healthy, sane and vigorous person herself she was almost obsessed by the dangers of inbreeding. Her only additions to the library at Tregear, apart from books on gardening, were the works of people like Galton, Weissman, Bateson and Müller—all concerned with the subject of inheritance as it was seen by the biologists of her generation. She never missed a chance to give me an object lesson on the virtues of outbreeding and what she called "the vigour of hybrids".'

A bracket clock on the mantelpiece chimed and struck ten, though it was half-past; a tabby cat came in from the garden, jumped on a chair and curled up to sleep. The atmosphere of the place was undemanding, the hours went by unmonitored by routine; with no deadlines. Clark chatted away about Amelia with a freedom which surprised me, and he spoke of his youth at Tregear with evident nostalgia.

'And yet, when she died, you sold up everything.'

He did not resent my remark but took time to consider his response.

'When Amelia died, Tregear died with her as far as I was concerned. I've been there only once since, and that was to collect a few things of a personal nature just before the sale. I am not in sympathy with the practice of embalming the past. Those rooms in the houses of the famous which have been preserved as they were when their owner lived send cold shivers down my spine. No society which believed in itself and its future would do such things.'

I liked him very much but I was plagued by the uncomfortable feeling that I had some deeply seated grudge against him and suddenly I understood why; he was an older version of Gordon

Clark, Charles's first cousin. Now I had realised it the resemblance seemed uncanny and I could not understand why I had not seen it at once.

He smoked his pipe for a while in silence, then he said, 'Of course the Clarks were only poor relations of the Bottrells but old Joseph did well by his in-laws. Not only did he take nephew Gordon into his business but he married him to his daughter, and Gordon eventually became a partner in the firm. When Elizabeth died Gordon married again and that's where I come in—I'm Gordon's grandson by his second marriage.' He grinned amiably.

I led the talk round to Charles.

'Was there no evidence as to what might have happened to him?'

He did not answer at once and when he did it seemed to me that he was deliberately non-committal. 'Amelia was very reluctant to talk about Charles but all through her life she insisted on the maze being maintained in good order and on fresh flowers being placed in a vase on the stone table.' He broke off, 'I suppose you know what I'm talking about—have you been in the maze?'

'Speak not evil of the dead, but call them blessed.'

He smiled. 'I see that you have. An enigmatic epitaph to say the least.'

'Wasn't there some talk of Charles having been murdered?'

'Possibly, but you must remember that all this happened before my time—a long time before.'

His manner was a mild rebuke, and I must have looked a little crestfallen for he made amends at once. 'All the same I can't pretend the subject wasn't still discussed in the family when I was a boy. There was talk of murder as you say and there seemed to be two schools of thought—one that he had got into a fight with gypsies and that they killed him . . .' He paused. 'The other was that grandfather was responsible.'

'Your grandfather?'

'Gordon. That, apparently, was the theory canvassed in the neighbourhood where he was less than popular, though I have never heard of any reason why Gordon should have killed his cousin other than a tale about a boyish squabble which ended in a rather bitter fight.'

'Isn't it more likely that Charles went off of his own accord?'

He nodded. 'I think so; from what I've heard of him he was something of a loner.'

With some hesitation I raised what might be another sensitive issue. 'It seems that Elizabeth was married exactly a month after her mother's death.'

'As soon as that, was it? I knew it wasn't long. A few eyebrows must have been raised.'

'And the bridegroom was only twenty; most middle-class young men of the time would have expected another eight to ten years of bachelorhood.'

Clark grinned. 'What are you saying? That the young couple beat the parson? It happened even in respectable Victorian families, but it must have been a bit embarrassing for poor old Joseph.'

'That's the point, really; they seem to have stirred up a lot of talk for nothing. Amelia was born, perfectly respectably, in due time after the wedding, on April 26th 1869.'

'My word! You have been doing your homework.'

I had the impression that he did not altogether approve, so I dropped the subject.

I mentioned that Lamb had loaned me a key and he seemed pleased rather than otherwise. 'Keep it for as long as you like. It's a good thing to have somebody about there, it will discourage vandals.'

'I would like to spend a few nights in the house.'

'Spend a month there if you want to, as long as you don't lay me open to pay rates on the place.'

We talked until almost twelve o'clock, and when I left I had a parcel of things which he said might interest me. 'I don't know exactly what's there, I've only glanced at a few of the letters. Let me have them back some time, but there's no great hurry.'

He came with me to the gate and I walked to the ferry with the parcel under my arm. Many of the boats which had been grounded when I arrived were now afloat.

I was pleased and relieved by my visit, for without his co-operation it would have been difficult if not impossible to carry out the rest of my plan. I drove back to Truro, parked the car and went to my bank, where I drew out most of what was in my account. I had a light lunch in a cafe, then started working through a shopping list which I had already prepared. I stocked up with dry goods and tinned stuff, enough I thought to last me a week. I took my purchases back to the car and drove to a camping shop on the quay, where I bought a sleeping bag, a butane stove and lamp, a kettle, a teapot, a couple of saucepans, a minimum of eating and drinking utensils and a good electric torch with a spare battery.

When all this was stowed away in the car I began to feel free.

My final act was to post a card to my mother which I had already written. It said, somewhat cryptically, 'I shall be out of touch for a few days but all is well, Bri.'

It was a fine afternoon, and when I arrived at Tregear I saw it under much the same conditions as on that first day. I drove into the stable yard, unlocked the plank door and unloaded my purchases, then I ran the car into the coach-house.

I decided to make my base in the old nursery, and when I had carted all my stuff upstairs I collected a lot of wood and brought it to the room next to the nursery, which was to be my fuel store. Whatever happened I was unlikely to suffer from cold, for there was an unlimited supply of wood on the estate. There was a pump in the yard which still worked and I found a couple of serviceable buckets but, as a precaution, I decided to boil all drinking water. All these preparations had diverted my thoughts from my main purpose, and I was beginning to feel like a boy scout with his eye on a whole set of badges.

I found a broken chair which was not too uncomfortable and a packing case to serve as a table, and I settled in. By this time it was five o'clock, and I had decided to take a look at the family graves in St Martin's churchyard.

Outside the sun still shone from an all but cloudless sky and it was warm. As I walked along the drive to the white gate I was alert for any possible change but nothing happened.

The Bottrells had a family vault but Elizabeth had not been

interred there. Her grave was with the Clarks' graves, a row of slate headstones near the west door. Hers was like the rest, inscribed with the IHS monogram and the usual details: 'In loving memory of Elizabeth, wife of Gordon Clark Bottrell, who departed this life May 16th 1884, aged 34 years.

'The life of the Spirit is eternal.'

The grave of Gordon's second wife was not there.

As I turned away a tall man with silvery hair and a bronzed complexion, and wearing a grey suit with a clerical collar, came out of the church. I introduced myself and told him of my interest in the Bottrells. 'I've been looking at their graves.'

'Perhaps you have been looking for someone who isn't there?' He had the manner of a mischievous schoolboy.

I explained that I knew about Charles.

He laughed. 'Ah, then you know of the family skeleton, so to speak! A strange business. When I came here forty years ago it was still a live topic of conversation among the villagers, at least among the older people.'

'What did they say?'

He frowned. 'Oh, it was only gossip.'

'They thought that Charles had been murdered?'

'That was the size of it, though nobody actually said so.'

'By the gypsies?'

His friendly grey eyes became suddenly very shrewd. 'My! You have been doing some research. I think the villagers were inclined to look for a culprit nearer home but I am quite sure that they hadn't the slightest justification. If you know anything about villages you won't need me to tell you that the more fantastic an idea is the more likely it is to gain currency—it becomes a sort of legend in which nobody really believes but everybody quotes.'

'You must have known Amelia.'

'Of course I knew her. I was going to say that I knew her in her prime, though she must have been close on seventy when I came here. No-one would have thought so. She was, and remained for many years, a vigorous woman and a force for good in the parish.'

'Apparently she was very insistent on her uncle's strange memorial being properly cared for . . .'

'Yes, indeed! That is quite true, which makes it all the more strange that she consistently refused to maintain her father's grave here in the churchyard. I broached the subject on more than one occasion and was promptly snubbed each time.' He laughed self-consciously. 'I gather that my predecessor had been similarly treated. You see, Mr Kenyon, how such an attitude might have been—indeed was, interpreted by the gossips.'

Now that I was free to spend as much time as I wished in the house I was reluctant to return there, and after leaving the church-yard I crossed to the pub which had just opened its doors. I drank half of lager standing at the bar, and got into conversation with the owner of the local garage who turned out to be an authority on the battles of the Civil War and an ardent Royalist. We had several drinks and it was quite dark when I left him.

For the first time I entered the grounds in darkness, and I was surprised that sounds which had been inaudible by day were now clear and distinct. I could hear the waterfall and even the swish of the sea over the shingle at the cove. An owl flew across the drive almost at the level of my eyes, silent and ghostly.

I am momentarily surprised by the orange glow which comes from several windows on the ground floor of the house. I raise the latch of the plank door and enter the kitchen to be greeted by familiar warm smells. Two of the maids are washing pots and pans at the sink, their sleeves rolled up over plump red arms. The eyes they turn on me are scared and I am puzzled, for they are ac-customed to me using the plank door whenever I wish to escape notice by the family.

'What's going on, Bowden?'

Bowden is the fatter of the two, and usually the more talkative, but she merely looks across the kitchen to Mrs Pascoe, the house-keeper, who is supervising preparations for dinner. Mrs Pascoe is a sour woman, and since my involvement with her niece, the Kenyon girl, she makes no secret of her dislike for me.

'The master wants you in the drawing-room, Mr Charles.'

It is impossible not to be aware of the tension in the atmosphere, the girls are going about their work with set faces and downcast eyes.

'Has something happened?'

'You must ask the master about that, Mr Charles.'

I have just come back from Trevessick where they have been digging out badgers, and I am in two minds whether I should change my clothes before going into the drawing-room, but her insistence decides me. I tap on the drawing-room door and go in. My father is standing with his back to the fireplace and there is no one else in the room. He looks pale and worried, and I have the impression that he has been pacing up and down waiting for me.

'Ah, there you are, Charles! I'm afraid that I have some distressing news. Late this afternoon your mother had another of her attacks; this one was worse than usual—very much worse—and, unfortunately, there was no one available to . . . to restrain her.'

I immediately conclude that mother has made another attempt on her life and that this time she has succeeded.

'Is she . . .?'

'She is not in any danger; set your mind at rest on that score. Your aunt and Dr Jordan are with her now, but she has been asking for you constantly, and Dr Jordan is of the opinion that you may be able to soothe her.'

'I will go to her.'

He holds up his hand, 'A moment, Charles! You have not heard all. While your mother is in this state of mental derangement she is not responsible for her actions, and this afternoon she attacked Elizabeth—'

'*Elizabeth!*' For the first time in my life I think that I may faint.

My father comes toward me. 'Elizabeth is going to be all right. Dr Jordan assures me that she will make a complete recovery.'

'But what happened?'

'By some means your mother obtained a kitchen knife which she secreted either in her room or about her person. This afternoon, when your aunt thought her to be asleep, she called Elizabeth to her bedside and attacked her. There was a struggle in which your sister received a deep wound in her left arm but, fortunately, she was able to break away. Your mother then turned the knife on herself, cutting her wrists.'

I feel cold inside. 'You are absolutely certain that Elizabeth is in no danger?'

I see my father's momentary change of expression an acknowledgement of my right to demand information as an equal.

'I assure you, Charles, a few days' rest and care and she will be well again.'

'Then I will go to mother.'

As I reach the door he calls after me. 'Your mother needs you, Charles; be charitable. Try to remember that only in her disturbed mental state would she dream of doing any harm to Elizabeth, whom she loves as we all do.'

My mother occupies a room at the far end of the corridor in the front of the house, her personal maid sleeps in the adjoining dressing-room, and my father has the room opposite. At night mother's door is locked so that she cannot leave her room without passing through the dressing-room. As I reach the landing I hear a low moaning sound. My mother is lying in bed with her eyes closed, and her arms, with the wrists bandaged, rest on the coverlet. She is deathly pale and she moans with each breath, but occasionally her lips move and she mutters unintelligible words.

Dr Jordan is seated on one side of the bed and aunt Florence on the other. Jordan has attended the family for more than forty years; he brought me and Elizabeth into the world and our brother who died in infancy. There are no secrets to which he is not privy. He is thin—so that his skin seems to be stretched over his bones— and he speaks in a dry, cracked voice.

'Speak to your mother, Charles.'

'Hullo, mamma.'

She opens her eyes and glares round the room with a wild staring expression which is frightening to see until her gaze rests on me, then there is a transformation; suddenly she is softer, younger, her eyes seem to brim over with love. 'Charles,' she murmurs, 'Charles.' But as her gaze shifts the look of madness returns and she becomes greatly excited, striving to articulate but almost frustrated by her passion. 'Get rid of them, Charles! Make them go!' Her left hand searches for mine and finds it, then, despite her wounded wrist, she holds my fingers with a grip that is painful. 'I don't want them here, Charles—any of them—only you.'

Then, with another abrupt change of mood, she is calm. She says with cool authority: 'I wish to talk to my son alone.'

Aunt Florence looks doubtfully at Dr Jordan but Jordan nods and gets up. 'Certainly, Mrs Bottrell, we will leave you to talk to Charles.'

The two of them go towards the dressing-room and my mother watches them with an expression of utter contempt. 'Fools! They understand nothing—nothing!' And a moment later she calls out: 'Shut that door! What I have to say to my son is private.'

When the door is closed she turns to me. 'Lie on the bed beside me, Charles.'

I do so, aware of the scent which my mother uses and which I have always found overwhelming, almost suffocating.

'Put your arms round me and kiss me.'

I have to confess that I am both frightened and repelled, but I do as I am told.

'On the lips, Charles . . . on the lips . . . Do I revolt you, Charles?'

'No, mamma, of course not!'

'I am thirty-seven, that's all—not an *old* woman.'

'No, mamma, of course you are not old.'

'Listen! We haven't much time for they will be back soon on some pretext or other.' She speaks in a voice that is little above a whisper. 'I tried to kill her this afternoon.'

I am resting on one elbow, looking down at her and I see her self-satisfied smile. 'I failed—or I think I did. I don't expect that she will die this time but I shall try again—when they least expect it. I shall kill her in the end.'

'But why, mamma? What has Elizabeth ever done to harm you? She loves you.'

'That's what she wants you to think. I knew you didn't understand. That's why I made them go away, so that I could explain. She's responsible, it is all her fault.'

'What is her fault?'

'My being as I am. It was when she was born. I knew it then, she took something away which belonged to me. I told them at 'In less than two years, Charles, you will have finished at She is smoothing my face with her right hand, running her fingers along the angle of my jaw and chin.

'From the time she was born I began to get ill and I've been getting worse, but it doesn't matter about me, it's you I worry about. She'll ruin your life, Charles, as she ruined mine. It's her or both of us, Charles, and when she goes all will be well—you'll see. We shall have the most wonderful times together.'

Her body suddenly goes limp and she sighs. 'I can't talk any more now, Charles. I'm tired, but you'll come again, won't you?'

'Yes, mother.'

'Promise?'

'I promise.'

I slide off the bed and move to the door of the dressing-room.

'You can tell them to come back now. And Charles—don't say anything to your father. He's taken in by her. It's a secret between us.'

I stand in the corridor for some time feeling truly ill. I want above everything to go to Elizabeth but I cannot trust myself, so I walk up and down for several minutes until I am calmer, then I tap on her door.

Elizabeth is propped up in bed, her left shoulder bare and her arm on that side swathed in bandages. Elsie Pope, our head parlourmaid, is sitting by the bed and she stands up as I come in.

'Do you want me to stay, sir?'

I shake my head and she leaves, closing the door behind her. We remain motionless, gazing at each other. I have never seen her look so lovely. Her black hair hangs down to her shoulders, emphasising the whiteness of her skin, and her eyes seem enormous. There are tears in them and she speaks in a whisper.

'Charles!'

'Elizabeth!'

I am lying across her body and she is fondling my hair with her free hand. I turn to look up into her face and she bends to kiss me on the lips. My arm is around her and we lie, kissing wildly, until our faces are hot and wet with tears.

'I shall hurt your arm, dearest.'

'It doesn't matter, nothing matters now'

CHAPTER SEVEN .

I OPENED MY eyes to a room flooded with sunshine; I looked up at the flaking ceiling and at the moulded cornice, and wondered where I was, then I became aware of the texture of the sleeping bag in contact with my skin, of the fireplace filled with wood-ash, of my belongings in little heaps on the floor, and I remembered. But as I lay there my most vivid recollections belonged not to me but to Charles Bottrell. It was not the graveyard at St Martin or my conversation with the vicar which came most readily to mind, it was the oppressive atmosphere of the room in which Charles's mother lay, her morbid obsession, her frightening smile, and above all contact with her moist, cold skin. It was Elizabeth and that first kiss on the lips followed by an embrace through which the pure essence of love seemed to flow. Memories that were not really mine at all.

It occurred to me that I could not recall any transition, I had no idea when, or in what circumstances, I had repossessed myself. If I had experienced the usual nausea, the shuddering and exhaustion, I had no memory of them.

I slid out of the sleeping bag and went down the corridor to the bathroom, where a sink and water closet worked well enough if I supplied water in buckets. I made coffee on my butane stove and ate cornflakes with tinned milk. The parcel of books and papers which Clark had given me remained unopened on my packing-case table. At the moment I felt in no need of documents, I had been in too close contact with the reality of the past.

I went out by the plank door, round the house to the terrace, and down the steps. The park was at its spring best; all the deciduous trees were dressed overall in lime green, bluebells were opening before the primroses had gone, ferns were unrolling young fronds, and everywhere there was the scent of moist, warm, regenerated earth.

Old man Blight, working at his saw-bench, gave me a greeting. 'Still about, then?'

'For a few days longer.'

He shrugged. 'Every man to his taste.'

I went through the kissing-gate and out into the cove. There was nobody to be seen, but a mongrel dog sniffed along the margins of the shore. In one of those cottages Molly Couch had lived with her cuckolded husband, another had been in the Blight family for three generations, spanning the century, and for most of that time Amelia Clark Bottrell had lived in the big house. And now it seemed that, in some strange way, it had fallen to me to bridge the gap of years.

I scrambled over the rocks to the nearby cove from which, it seemed, Charles and Gordon had usually bathed nude, or *al fresco*, as the Victorians had it. It was no more than a wedge of shingle between the rocks, backed by a fifty-foot cliff of shaley slate. At one point, for some forgotten reason, a vertical furrow had been cut in the face of the cliff through its whole height; the furrow was about three feet deep and less than two in width. This must have been the 'chimney' which the children had spoken of. It was quite a practicable climb but by no means easy for youngsters with a short reach, and for Elizabeth, hampered by skirts and long drawers, it must have been an ordeal indeed.

A few small craft dotted the sea, and way out a big ship was steaming down-channel.

I walked slowly back the way I had come and re-entered the park by the kissing-gate. I passed Blight with a word and walked up the stream until I reached the maze. I had not been in the maze alone since my bizarre game of hide and seek with Charles, but I had no fear of anything of the kind happening again. If at that time our two personalities had been in conflict, it was now as though they were beginning to merge. I found my way to the centre of the maze, hampered by the unpruned branches which were just as I had left them after cutting my way through with the billhook. I went into the little building and stood by the table which bore Charles's epitaph.

Quite suddenly, from one moment to the next, the building was gone and I was out in the open, the surface of the table, now quite smooth, gleaming in the sunlight. The hedges were clipped, the gravelled paths were free of weeds, the maze was no longer secret and sinister, but a place of amusement for idle people on long summer afternoons.

After glancing up to the rocky platform to make sure that I am not observed, I stoop and look under the table. Where one of the carved stone legs joins the top there is a recess, and in the recess there is a folded piece of paper. I take it out, unfold it and read what is on it.

'And we will live like two birds in one nest—

Enid.

'He marks how well the ship her helm obeys . . .'

It is a foolish little game which Elizabeth and I play. I quote a line from her favourite poet, Tennyson, and she has to quote the next line and give the name of the poem. She then chooses a line from my favourite, Byron, and I have to add the next line and identify the poem. It is an unwritten law that we never speak of it. If one of us finds a quotation difficult the other may have to go to the table on several days before finding a piece of paper in the niche. It is considered ignominious to 'give in.'

I identify the *Corsair* at once, but I shall have to locate the quotation before I can give the next line. Recently I have tried hard to find quotations to which her rejoinder will look like a profession of love.

I leave the maze and climb the slope past the waterfall. The scrap of paper makes me feel sad, it is a link with our childhood and a symbol of our youth together; the one is gone and the other is threatened by each day that passes. We can never be closer than we are at this time

I could go to our day-room to look up the quotation, but I go instead to the library, knowing that Elizabeth will be there with Jollibones.

They are head to head over Virgil; Elizabeth's dark tresses against his yellow fuzz. Elizabeth's arm is out of the sling and she is wearing a new morning dress of some blue stuff with puffed sleeves. The bodice is tight and accentuates her little breasts. I wonder if her nearness excites Jollibones. Although he is such a dry stick he cannot be more than twenty-eight or nine.

'Virgil is a poet of the countryside, he was born and reared in the country. The Eclogues and The Georgics in particular . . .'

Jollibones catches sight of me and breaks off. He has never liked me. Elizabeth looks up and smiles, the world is suddenly a better place. I shall try to arrange for us to go sailing together on Saturday.

I find my quotation in Byron's *Corsair*: 'He marks how well the ship her helm obeys, How gallant all her crew and deigns to praise.'

I leave them and go up to our day-room to sit, staring out of the window, thinking nothing. My sketchbook is open on the table in front of me and I flick through the pages. All the sketches are of buildings or of animals, the buildings are, most of them, imaginary and many are absurd. *Design for a Royal Rabbit Hutch* portrays a very ornate building in the Gothic style, surmounted by the Royal Arms, with a rabbit peering out of each of the windows. Another is a crazy little building which looks like a cross between a pagoda and a church tower. It has battlements and little animals at the corners instead of gargoyles. Underneath it I have written: 'In loving memory of C.J.B. Esq. of Tregear.' That must have been one of my black days.

I wonder how my father manages. I cannot remember the time when he slept in the same room as my mother. Does he go to the house in Goodwives Lane? He would never take the risk of being seen, least of all by me. Mrs Pascoe? It would be against his principles so to conduct himself in the house. There must be somewhere very discreet, where, perhaps, the gentlemen wear masks or perform through suitable screens.

It occurs to me as a good thing that I shall probably not live long. Given time I could become the wickedest man in the world.

Since that evening in her room Elizabeth has become more remote, more circumspect; as gentle and fond as ever, but we have become aware of barriers, invisible yet monstrous ramparts guarding against dangers we did not know before.

I made some coffee and unpacked the parcel which Clark had given me. There were several mounted photographs, a box of letters, a couple of fat notebooks, and three ledgers which made up the bulk of the parcel, the household accounts of Tregear over sixty years. They would have been of great value to a genuine historian but they were of no interest to me now. I was no longer concerned with the history of Tregear nor, indeed, with the Bottrell family, only with the lives of Charles and Elizabeth.

Of the dozen photographs I picked out two; one showed Charles, Elizabeth and Gordon, posed on the steps leading to the terrace in front of the house. Elizabeth must have been seventeen or eighteen at the time, and Charles, very little taller than his sister, might easily have been her twin. Charles looked at the camera with sullen distaste while Gordon, towering above them both and smiling broadly, looked more like a young farm-hand than a member of the family. The second photograph both fascinated and repelled me; it was a wedding picture of Elizabeth and Gordon, taken outside the church. However rational I tried to be I found it impossible to look at the photograph without being disturbed by the notion that here was a preliminary to rape.

I turned to the notebooks—*Amelia Clark-Bottrell's Common Place Book, 1882-1890,* and a second volume of the same dated 1891-1900.

The early entries were written in a childish hand and consisted mainly of poems and passages of prose copied from edifying books, but occasionally there was a paragraph or two of spontaneous writing, an account of a birthday, a notable visit, an excursion or a disappointment. Later the book became more of a journal, though the entries were sporadic and often cryptic. I skimmed the pages, for the drama which interested me had been played out before Amelia was born and I had little expectation from her book. I was wrong.

On May 16th 1884 Amelia recorded her mother's death with curiously objective detachment. 'Today dearest mamma passed away after being confined to her bed for three weeks. She had never fully recovered from a chill contracted in the late autumn, and throughout the winter her health steadily declined. Despite all that the doctors could do she lost weight and became increasingly listless, so that Dr Borlase once remarked to papa in my hearing: "Your wife seems to have lost the will to live." During the past three weeks she has been racked by spasms of coughing which her medicine did little to relieve.'

A few days later she wrote: 'Papa appears to find consolation in being much occupied with business, but dear grandpapa is beside himself with grief and I do what I can to comfort him.'

Two years after her mother's death her father married again: 'I have no reason to regard the lady with other than kindness, but I have no taste for the rôle of stepdaughter, and as it is grandpapa's wish that I shall remain with him I shall certainly do so. I do not think that my decision will be greatly regretted by papa and his wife.'

From many entries it was clear that Joseph did all he could to give his granddaughter every advantage which wealth and affection could provide, and Amelia wrote of him with increasing fondness. Towards the end of the first book, when she was in her late teens, there were occasional, rather amused, references to his attempts at matchmaking. 'I think that dear grandpapa had hopes of that young gentleman . . .' and, 'At breakfast grandpapa asked me, with an appearance of casualness; "Did you not form a good opinion of young Mr Fox?" '

But as recorded in the very last entry of the first book, dear grandpapa died. 'It came suddenly, with no warning, while he was sitting in his wicker chair on the terrace, taking the morning air . . . Dr Borlase says that it was an affection of the heart and he assures me that there was no pain. I weep for him as I write, for during these last years he has been to me father, mother and loving, generous friend. I owe him everything I am and have.'

Amelia, now of age, and wealthy, took her responsibilities seriously. She appears to have gone through her grandfather's papers with meticulous care. Three months after the funeral she wrote:

'I have not had the courage to write in this book for more than a week, since, indeed, the discovery which now weighs so heavily upon me and which I cannot, dare not share with another living soul. Fortunately I did not allow Mr Bawden to take away those of grandpapa's papers which were of a more personal or intimate nature, and I have spent some time in going through them. There is a great quantity, for grandpapa kept a note of even the smallest happenings affecting the family and the estate, and I was greatly moved to discover that everything concerning the family is recorded in the most affectionate and indulgent manner possible. He did not keep a diary or journal, but wrote on odd sheets of paper which he then placed in unsealed envelopes dated on the outside with the period to which they referred.

'Among these papers I came across a sealed envelope addressed to him in my mother's hand which bore the instruction: "In case of my death to be handed to Amelia when she reaches mature age." I was not prepared, nor could I possibly have been, for the horror which the contents disclosed.

'For a time I was beside myself and feared that I might not be able sufficiently to conceal my distress from those around me. I cannot believe that dear grandpapa would willingly have subjected me to this shock, and I must conclude that he was ignorant of those facts which it was my birthright to know, of which I should have been informed by my mother before her death.

'It is well that I had previously had doubts about the wisdom of marriage, and I thank God that I have formed no attachment for any member of the opposite sex. On the day after reading mamma's papers I burned them in the fireplace in my room, not content until every charred fragment had been reduced to dust. I could fancy, I suppose in self-pity, that it was my life which had been thus consumed.'

There was a break of more than two months during which Amelia did not write in her book, and when she resumed making more or less regular entries it was clear that she had come to terms with her distress and with its cause.

'After this lapse of time I begin to see mamma's revelations in a different light, and I realise that it is not only wrong but pointless to harbour bitterness. We are all human and, in some degree, victims of circumstance. At least I feel that I understand mamma better. She had room in her life for only one love; for me there was kindness, even tenderness, but no love. Seen through the eyes of one less deeply involved than I, it is possible that there might have been something fine in her tragic obsession, perverted though it was.

'I am glad that I know and can accept the truth. It would be easy for me, in self-pity, to sustain the notion that my life has been blighted, but, in honesty, I cannot believe that its course will be very much changed. I had already come near to the conclusion that I am not of the marrying kind. Marriage either gives too little or demands too much.

'But if I can find it in my heart to forgive mamma I have little charity to spare for the man I believed to be my father, whose motives were of an altogether meaner sort.'

I put the book aside. I seemed to have lost all sense of the passage of time and my watch had stopped. I turned to the little radio I had brought with me and switched it on.

'There is a growing feeling among the political parties that an autumn election is on the cards. If the short-term economic indicators remain favourable it is likely that the prime minister will feel tempted to go to the polls—'

I switched it off again. As far as I was concerned the man could have been speaking in Swahili.

That morning I saw a young couple in the grounds; they stood by the ornamental pond looking up at the house. Obviously they had climbed the white gate or evaded Blight's vigilance at the cove. They took a snap of the house, then wandered off in the direction of the waterfall. I wondered if there were any ghosts for them.

At some time I felt hungry and made myself a full meal. I opened a tin of sausages, and fried and ate them with boiled potatoes. Dusk was spreading across the park and out over the sea by the time I had finished. I lit my lamp, made coffee and started to write my notes.

Molly is expecting me; Billy will be out all night fishing. It is a flat calm with no moon and the only sound comes from the water rippling across the sand. The Couches live in the end cottage and a faint scratching on the door is enough. I hear her moving inside the cottage, then the door opens with scarcely a creak. The oil lamp is lit but turned low. Molly wears only her shift; we do not speak. She closes the door and turns up the lamp. The room is warm from the heat of the stove, there is always plenty of wood for the cottagers. The floor in front of the stove is covered with an assortment of mats, blankets and old coats—God knows what else. I asked her once why we could not use the bed upstairs and got a sharp answer:

'I draws the line at that, Mr Charles! Not his bed!'

I put my arms round her and feel the velvet smoothness of her body under the calico, but she is impatient of preliminaries and pulls her shift off.

'Get undressed, do!'

Her breasts are large and heavy, her hips broad and voluptuous, she is eager, wild and shameless, with a lewd tongue—the very stuff of a young man's erotic dreams.

'You are good to me, Molly.'

She chuckles. 'I don't do it for your benefit, that's for sure; nor for the shilling or two you gives me.'

'Aren't you afraid that I shall give you another baby, Molly?'

'What of it? If you don't, he will. As long as the poor little bastard has black hair it don't signify.'

We are lying side by side, exhausted, and she is staring up at the smoke-blackened ceiling beams. 'Billy is a good man but the chapel got 'old of 'n. He feels guilty about it; keeps his nightshirt on an' I got to wear me shift. An' I ain't allowed to talk.'

I stroke her belly, down to the black triangle.

'You've had more 'n enough o' that for one night, Mr Charles; you still got to walk back.'

'Are all women like you underneath, Molly?'

'I s'pose so, they all got the same as I got though you wouldn' think so to look at some of 'em.'

'I meant, do they all feel the same?'

She raises herself on one elbow and looks down at me, smiling. 'You're a queer one. 'Ow should I know how they feel? I reckon a woman 'as to be woke up, so to speak, an' some sleep sounder 'n others.' She laughs so that her breasts shake. 'Why? Is there a special woman in your mind?'

'No, certainly not.'

'Then you should be thinking about it; this don't lead nowhere for a young man in your position.'

'I shall never marry, Molly.'

She laughs again. 'Where've I 'eard that before?'

I stand up and start groping for my clothes while she watches me with frank interest.

'Nobody would think to look at you that you could give a woman much. Sometimes I think 'tis the little 'ns as are best at it.' After a moment she adds, 'My little black an' white monkey—that's what you are; just like a little black an' white monkey.'

I start to dress.

'How do you manage when you're away to Oxford?'

'I do without.'

'I bain't daft enough to believe that, Mr Charles, but you watch out, you need to be careful in they places.'

As I walk back through the park in the darkness it is starting to rain, great heavy drops which strike the foliage audibly. The house is still and warm and filled with a long familiar pattern of smells. I feel like a predatory animal returning to its lair; sometimes I wish that I could live wholly within myself, unaccountable and unaccounted.

I woke to hear the rain beating against the window and I lay in my sleeping bag watching the water cascading down the panes. I wondered vaguely what day it was, for I could not remember how many nights I had slept in the house. The record I was to have

114

made of my stay had not progressed beyond a few lines. Time passed, night succeeded day, and though I seemed to do very little I was never conscious of being idle. I suspect that I spent a lot of time day-dreaming. From the first my excursions into the life of Charles Bottrell had recaptured episodes which were isolated and largely inconsequential; there was rarely any coincidence of hour or season, and now it seemed that my own life was breaking loose from its established rhythms, and that in some strange and not unpleasant way I had been cast adrift.

I got up, boiled an egg and ate it with some cracker biscuits, for the bread which I had brought with me had gone stale. By that time the rain had cleared and the sun was breaking through.

I walked slowly down through the estate where trees and shrubs were still dripping from the rain and it was soft under foot. I let myself out through the kissing-gate into the deserted cove and walked along to the end cottage, where I stood for a while looking at the closed door and the curtained windows, then I wandered along the shore. It was easy to believe that I had crept out of that door only a few hours before; Molly, still naked, holding the latch. A lewd parting gesture and a suppressed giggle.

I walked back to the house because I had nothing else to do, and as I came out of the shrubbery I saw a girl on the terrace. At first I thought that she was just another sight-seer, then I recognized Karen. I think that I might have hidden, but she saw me and came down the steps. Her manner was tentative, diffident, obviously she was not sure what reception she would get.

'So I've run you to earth.'

'How did you manage it?'

'I guessed. Monica Turner said she saw you on Monday afternoon, coming out of the camp shop looking like a Christmas tree.'

Monica Turner was a teacher of physical education at the school. Karen imitated her to perfection.

'I didn't know that Brian was an open-air type. In any case, isn't he supposed to be ill?'

'I don't care a damn about Monica Turner.'

'Neither do I but Mason is bound to hear through the grape vine.'

'To hell with Mason.'

She looked at me. 'Sorry I spoke.'

We were walking round the house to the yard at the back. 'Anyway, why aren't you at school?'

'Because it's Saturday. For God's sake, Brian, don't you know what day it is? What's happened to you?'

'Nothing has happened to me. I wanted to spend a few days in the house alone; I got permission from the owner, and that's all there is to it.'

'But you've lost weight and you've got a week's growth of beard.'

'I'm sorry, I would have spruced myself up if I had expected a visitor.'

There was a little red sports car in the yard.

'I borrowed it from Tim Birch.'

'I hope this isn't going to turn into a sort of menagerie with the staff making weekend excursions.'

She stopped short. 'Why the hell I bother about you, God knows! I've told nobody that I thought you were here, and I shall tell nobody that you are. You can stay here as far as I'm concerned until you bloody well rot. I brought a few things I thought you might be glad of, but if you don't want them or me just say the word.'

I reached out and held her hand. 'Sorry.'

'So you should be. Where do you sleep?'

'In the nursery.'

'The nursery?'

'One of the front rooms on the first floor.'

'You'd better give me a hand.'

I was embarrassed by the amount of food she had brought and her concern, but we carried the stuff through the kitchens and up the stairs to the nursery. She looked round with a critical eye.

'At least you can keep yourself warm.' After a moment she added; 'Am I allowed to stay and have lunch with you?'

'Of course—what time is it?'

'Haven't you got a watch?'

'I haven't bothered with it.'

'Well, it's just gone twelve. I'll get something.' She began by throwing wood on the fire, causing it to blaze up.

She had brought a whole chicken, already cooked, now she boiled potatoes and greens, and we ate, sharing a fork.

'I brought a bottle of plonk to wash it down, but if you're doing a hermit act . . .'

We relaxed.

'I suppose you've no idea when you will be back?'

'I need a few more days.'

I made coffee, and afterwards we sat on the sleeping bag in front of the fire. Karen had taken off her coat and was wearing a linen dress which zipped down the front. I fingered the zip.

'Do you want to?'

I nodded.

She slipped out of her dress and lay by my side in brassière and briefs. I slid my hand inside her briefs and thought of Molly. At that moment Elizabeth was in the nursery with us. The room had not changed, it was still bare and anonymous with my meagre and makeshift belongings scattered around, but Elizabeth was there, standing by the door, watching us with an expression of astonishment and contempt. She was dressed as I had never seen her before, and never had I seen her looking more beautiful. She wore a white gown, slightly off the shoulders, with a low décolletage and decorated with lace edgings, flounces and artificial flowers. Her wonderful hair was caught up in a chignon at the nape of her neck, restrained by a fine net laced with pearls. She wore white gloves and in her left hand she carried a fan. I was mesmerised.

'Aren't you going to undress?'

'What?'

'Aren't you going to take your clothes off?'

I withdrew my hand. 'Sorry, Karen, I can't.'

She pulled up her briefs and reached for her dress.

'I am really very sorry, Karen.'

'Why the hell should I care?'

She zipped up her dress and picked up her coat, and a moment later I heard her footsteps on the stairs. I waited until I heard the roar of the little sports car being revved at high speed and my only feeling was one of escape.

CHAPTER EIGHT

SATURDAY IS FINE and warm with the tides just right, and father has agreed that we may go sailing if John Trevail considers it safe. By nine o'clock in the morning we are already at the cove and Trevail has the boat in the water, her blunt bow nosing the shingle. She is really no more than a heavy, beamy rowing boat with a mast stepped just aft of the bow thwart, and she carries a big brown lug-sail which is easy to handle.

'There's a bit of a breeze out o' the nor-west. You run wi' the tide down toward the Nare an' you can put in where you 'ave a mind to. Then, if you leave it till fivish before starting 'ome, the wind 'll most likely back a bit an' you'll come 'ome han'some wi' wind and tide.'

Elizabeth is wearing a plain grey dress like the village girls and a straw hat with a broad brim. Molly Couch is at her door watching us, her baby in her arms.

I use the sweeps to get clear of the cove, then hoist the old patched sail. She finds the breeze and water begins to chuckle under the bow. Elizabeth takes the tiller. We have been out many times with Trevail and I often sail alone or with Gordon, but this is the first time I have been entrusted with Elizabeth, alone.

'Happy?'

She grins.

We do not hug the coast, but we are close enough to recognize all the landmarks we know so well. The breeze from the north-west is quite strong, but soon we begin to feel the shelter of the Nare and also the strength of the sun.

We decide to land at Kiberick, a rocky cove in the neck of the headland. It is enclosed on three sides by fairly steep cliffs and, seen from the sea, the rocks and the grey sand are backed by an almost solid wall of brilliant yellow gorse. We go about and steer for the beach so that the old boat just brushes the sand before losing way completely. Elizabeth picks up her skirts and jumps ashore. I pass her the picnic basket, then I balance our little anchor on the bows and go ashore with a line tied to one of its flukes. We push the boat off, and when she is fifteen yards or so from the shore a tug on the line dislodges the anchor which falls into the water with a good splash; we hope that it will hold.

'It doesn't matter if she grounds, we shall just have to stay here until she floats again.'

We both know that it is going to be one of those rare days when everything goes right. The cove is idyllic, completely sheltered, and even on the beach the scent of the gorse is strong. I find a piece of drift wood and hammer it into the sand with the help of a rock to secure our anchor line. To make assurance doubly sure Elizabeth piles big stones round the post.

Satisfied, we walk along the tide-line looking for anything which has been washed up. We find a couple of purple jellyfish, several mermaid's purses, some whelks' eggs and a string of corks which has been used to mark somebody's lobster pots. There is a tidal pool among the rocks to the east of the cove, and we spend some time watching the anemones and sea-squirts.

'Shall we bathe?'

It is not the first time Elizabeth and I have bathed together, me in my drawers and Elizabeth in her chemise and drawers. They have to be dried afterwards, but if the servants ever notice that they have been in salt water we never hear of it. Elizabeth finds a nook in which she can undress as modestly as possible, and when she comes out I am already in the water.

'Don't watch me, Charles, *please!*'

She has tied her hair in a knot on the top of her head. We swim round the boat like excited children. Elizabeth swims very well considering how little practice she gets, and I show off by diving under the boat, swimming under water for a time, then coming up and tickling her feet. A wonderful day.

Afterwards we sit on the beach to get dry. Elizabeth lets her hair down and we eat our picnic meal—cold chicken and ham, bread, slices of seed cake and a bottle of very light wine which father regards as almost non-alcoholic. By the time we have eaten, our underclothes have dried on us. The moment is passing; soon it will be too late.

'Elizabeth . . .'

'Yes, Charles?'

'Let me see you without your clothes.'

She looks at me very solemnly. 'You really want to?'

'Yes.'

'Have you ever seen a girl . . .?'

'Yes.'

She is very serious and her lower lip trembles. 'Will you promise not to touch me?'

'I promise.'

'You must *not* touch me, Charles.'

'No.'

'All right, look away.'

I do as she wishes.

'Now.'

She is beautiful beyond my imagining, not voluptuous, not sensual but chaste and exquisite.

'Move your hands.'

She does so.

'Now you, Charles.' Her voice has an unfamiliar huskiness.

'But surely you must have seen boys bathing . . .'

'I have; I want to see you.'

I would give my life to trace with my finger the profile of her breasts.

'I love you, Elizabeth.'

'I love you, Charles, but we must never do this again.' She shivers as she says this.

'Are you cold?'

'No of course not.'

We dress and explore the cliffs, working our way round to the very tip of the Nare, and when we return to the beach the boat is aground so we sit on the sand to wait for the tide to refloat her.

'In less than two years, Charles, you will have finished at university; what shall you do then?'

I am tracing patterns in the sand with my finger and do not answer.

'Shall you work with father as he expects?'

'No.' I draw an almost perfect circle. 'In two years you may well be married.'

She shakes her head. 'Not in two years, but I suppose that I shall marry one day. There is no alternative for a woman.'

'But if we both remain single there would be no reason why we should not live together. It often happens that a single or widowed man has his sister to keep house for him; it is accepted.'

'Would that be enough for you, Charles?'

'I would make it enough.'

'It would not be enough for me, Charles, and more is not possible.'

I am astonished at the incisiveness of her reply and not at all sure that I fully understand her thoughts.

We are speaking of two years and more ahead, yet I cannot really believe in such a time. I have had strange experiences of late which seem to cast some glimmer of light on that future which has both beckoned and threatened me since childhood. Most often these experiences come at night. I seem to wake and there is a man at my bedside. He is strangely dressed and I feel that I know him though I cannot give him a name. I am aware of a deep bond between us. We do not speak but ideas seem to pass, ideas vague and ill-defined as a puff of smoke, yet when he is gone I feel that I know a little more and it frightens me.

'Charles!'

'What is it?'

'The boat is afloat, you've been asleep.'

We sail home as John Trevail said that we would, running before wind and tide.

After Karen's visit it was not long before I had once more lost count of the hours and days so that I was sometimes wandering about the estate at night. I had become so familiar with the place that darkness made little difference to me, and though I had no idea of any purpose in these wanderings, neither have I any recollection of being bored. I ate when I was hungry and slept when I was tired; I no longer saw any need to continue with what I had regarded as an investigation, I had no inclination to find out more about the house or the family or even about Charles Bottrell and my relationship with him. It was enough that I should be identified with him, and it was as though all my curiosity, my strength of purpose and, indeed, my capacity for emotion had somehow drained away from my life into his.

One morning when I had run out of bread, potatoes and biscuits I decided that I must go to the little shop in the village. It seemed a momentous decision, and I put it off several times. I looked at myself in my shaving mirror and was shocked by what I saw; my face was thin to the point of emaciation and I had several days' growth of beard. The collar of my shirt was filthy, and looking down at my pullover and slacks I saw that they, too, were dirty and snagged. I spent some time washing and shaving. Fortunately I still had a couple of clean shirts and a spare pair of trousers which I had not worn since my arrival. I dressed myself and felt like a convalescent who wears his normal clothes again after a long spell in pyjamas and dressing gown. At the last moment I remembered that I needed money and took my wallet from the mantelpiece.

It was a windless day with a sea mist drifting in, condensing and dripping from the trees. The little village shop was called a 'mini-market' and I had to stand in a queue of housewives with my wire basket, feeling like a man from Mars.

Outside I was hailed by the vicar and the ambiguity of my position was brought home to me.

'You haven't come to live with us?'

'What? No, I came to take another look at the house and thought I would buy a few things.'

It sounded thin and he looked at me oddly but made no further comment.

I walked back to the house with my bag full of purchases and went up to the nursery, where the packing-case desk was littered with books, letters, papers and photographs—all of which had seemed so important to me only a short while before. I threw some wood on the fire and sat staring at the flames. I supposed that it must be time for a meal but I did nothing about it, and it is probable that I fell asleep.

There is a tap on the door and a maid comes in. 'The master says will you take your place in the hall now, please sir.'

I put on my jacket and adjust my tie. 'Is Miss Elizabeth down there?'

'Miss Elizabeth is already in the hall, sir.'

It is traditional that Elizabeth and I receive the guests for Christmas dinner which is at three in the afternoon. The hall is festive, with a tall Christmas tree, decorated and lit with candles, and there is a wood fire burning in the grate. The front door stands open but the inner, glass doors are closed. I can see Parsons and the stable boy out on the steps, waiting to take care of the horses. My place is to the right as the guests arrive, with Richards, the butler, behind me. Elizabeth stands to the left with Pope, the head parlourmaid, behind her. It is the same every year and has been since I can remember, though I have no idea how the custom arose. In any case Christmas dinner is only for the family and the vicar.

The clock on the landing shows three minutes to two o'clock. Father and mother and aunt Florence are in the drawing-room. Mamma has been remarkably well for the past few days, and for the first time in three years, she is to take her place at the Christmas table.

Elizabeth is wearing her afternoon dress of pale blue silk with dark blue fringes. She has a little more colour than usual and she looks across at me and smiles, that smile which is both intimate and mysterious. How I love her!

The clock makes its usual throat-clearing noises, then strikes two. Almost at once the vicar's gig arrives. My father and the vicar disagree strongly on church matters, but the appearances are always preserved. Richards and Pope open the glass doors and Mr Sandfield comes in with his wife; their children are already grown up and have left the nest. They are relieved of their top-coats and Mrs Sandfield is escorted by a maid to the ladies' retiring room, while I lead the vicar to the drawing-room and the Madeira which is his favourite tipple.

The day is crisp and cold, with sunshine, and I wish that Elizabeth and I could be tramping over the cliffs instead of performing these meaningless rituals. God alone knows how much time we have left.

Gordon's parents, uncle Arthur and aunt Amelia Jane, arrive in their dog-cart.

'The young people decided to walk, it is such extremely clement weather.'

Why aunt Amelia Jane should trouble to keep up such pretension with us is a mystery. We know the struggle they have to maintain a horse and dog-cart, let alone a carriage which would accommodate the whole family. But she is both earnest and feather-brained, so that she makes the noises she has been trained to make whether they are appropriate or not.

'My *dear* Elizabeth! What a charming young lady you have become, to be sure.'

Uncle Arthur is a big man, large and ineffective, who says foolish things with an air of great profundity. 'Just think, Charles my boy, in a week, in only seven days it will be Anno Domini eighteen hundred and sixty-eight!'

Jollibones arrives on foot, in the same coat as always, green and shining with age. With his long thin neck, small head and crop of very fair hair he looks like a plucked chicken.

'Miss Elizabeth, Mr Charles.' I am sure that he blushes as he speaks to Elizabeth.

Finally, Gordon with his younger brother, John, who has a slight hare-lip, and his sister, Priscilla, who is the same age as Elizabeth. All three of them are big, with a kind of lumpishness as though they have been carelessly moulded out of clay. Gordon, now that he is in the bank, makes a greater effort with his appearance but still manages to look like a prosperous young farmer. He and I are reconciled, though he still has a white scar on his upper lip as a memento of our fight.

Elizabeth goes off with Priscilla while I take the two boys into the drawing-room, where everybody is on their best behaviour and mamma is surreptitiously eyed by all except poor Jollibones, who, with a glass in his hand, sits staring at the carpet.

Promptly at three o'clock Richards announces dinner and we go in. Apart from mamma's presence it is the same as the year before and the years before that. The talk turns to depression in the mines, depression in agriculture, mob violence in Redruth and distress in the clay-pits.

Aunt Amelia Jane announces that she is on a committee with certain titled personages who are setting up a soup kitchen in St Austell for the families of the clay workers.

'The soup will be sold at the very low price of one penny per quart.'

Uncle Arthur clears his throat and says with great gravity: 'Whether or not that is a low price depends, in my opinion, on the nutritive value of the soup.'

Richards brings in the Christmas pudding wreathed in phantom brandy flames and it is ceremoniously served.

'We are delighted to see you so well again, Mary,' aunt Amelia Jane says to my mother while the rest of us hold our breaths. 'It must have been very difficult for Joseph during the past two or three years. I cannot *imagine* how Arthur and the children would manage without me. You were so fortunate in being able to call upon dear Florence.'

Mamma appears to take it calmly; she is in the act of helping herself to cream from a dish held by a maid. She replaces the spoon in the dish, nods to the maid, then turns to my aunt.

'Yes, indeed; we are grateful to Florence. I am sure that she has done everything possible; certainly all that I could have done, including sharing my husband's bed.'

The silence, for a moment, is absolute, then aunt Amelia Jane lets out a foolish little laugh and says: 'But that is quite absurd, Mary, my dear. Florence is his sister-in-law.'

Mamma, still calm, says very quietly and distinctly: 'His *widowed* sister-in-law.'

The vicar raises a spoonful of pudding to his lips. 'This is a most extraordinarily good pudding.' He looks across the table to his wife. 'I think that it must be the nutmeg. You should try adding a little nutmeg to your recipe, my dear. I can definitely taste the nutmeg.'

For a moment, at least, the situation is saved; conversation breaks out again and after a little while mamma rises in a perfectly natural manner and invites the ladies to join her in the drawing-room. Elizabeth gives me a backward despairing glance.

As often before I am amazed at our capacity to absorb shocks when to do otherwise would be inconvenient. Even aunt Florence holds her tongue.

Somehow the time passes. We have presents off the Christmas tree; mamma plays the piano, accompanying the vicar in a solo which he sings in a thin tenor. Elizabeth and Priscilla sing a duet in which Elizabeth takes the soprano and Priscilla the contralto with very pleasing effect. We play some tedious round games and then, with a cold supper at ten o'clock, it is over.

We see them off, standing on the steps in the clear, crisp night air. Elizabeth is wearing a pale blue shawl which matches her dress. When they have gone I fetch my top coat and walk down through the park in the moonlight. I reach the rock platform and stand looking down at the maze where the gravelled paths stand out in a pale ghostly pattern. I continue down the slope and enter the maze.

I know that he is here; it was in the maze that I first actually *saw* him. Before that I was afraid because I believed him to be hostile, and when I am afraid I become aggressive. I know that I frightened him. I saw him through a thin place in the hedge, and after that we seemed to draw closer and to achieve an increasing rapport. On that occasion our hands almost touched, and I had the absurd impression that I was seeing myself in a mirror. In a mirror one can never actually touch one's own image, there is always a gap.

He is standing by the stone table. For an instant, as I reach the centre, I have the impression of a little building. Of course, it is a trick of the moonlight; but my friend is there right enough. I think of him now as my friend—more than a friend. His dress is strange, he wears a short coat of some shiny material with a furry collar and he is hatless, as I am. He seems to be looking straight at me. Sometimes I have felt that he knows me better than I know myself and that he has some message for me which he cannot communicate. At other times it seems that we are both striving to look into a future which is dark and troubled.

As I move toward him he disappears. I can no longer see him but I know that he is close, very close. I stand by the stone table looking down at it and suddenly I am afraid, though not of him.

CHAPTER NINE

As I BEGIN to write of my last days at Tregear my recollection becomes increasingly confused; I am no longer able to distinguish clearly between the times when I thought and felt and behaved as Brian Kenyon and those other times when I lived the life of Charles Bottrell. All I can say is that my own life assumed less and less importance, restricted, as it seemed to be, to intervals between episodes in the last few months of Charles's life. It is still the memories of his life in that period which are most real to me; my own have a dream-like quality with only an occasional incident held in sharp focus.

I suppose that it is the crux of my problem—of the shaman's problem—why, in fact, I am here in this institution. The ghost of Charles Bottrell must be exorcised if I am to fully recover my own identity—before, as the New Testament has it, I can be made whole. But the truth is that I do not want to lose my hold on the slender threads of that other life which meant more, means more, to me than my own.

'You are a man of high intelligence, an historian with a rich and vivid imagination. You have had a series of hallucinatory experiences —accept this simple fact and we shall be more than halfway to curing you.'

Swallow the jam and you won't notice the nasty powder.

If I was in the habit of using four-letter words I should probably do so at this point; instead I merely stare at them and shake my head.

All through I identified with Charles only when he was at home, never while he was away at school or, later, at Oxford. His life away from Tregear was and remains a blank for me, and the next and final phase of which I had any experience began four days after he came down for the long vacation of 1868.

I am out early, not long after daybreak.

This is our great day—the day of Tregear Fête which is held every year on the third Saturday in June. It happens this year to coincide with Elizabeth's eighteenth birthday, and Bottrell girls are considered as 'coming of age' at eighteen. The thought frightens me, the more so because yesterday evening aunt Florence remarked:

'Eighteen is a wonderful age, Elizabeth; it is the age at which a girl becomes *marriageable*, with all the joy which that implies. I married your late uncle when I was eighteen . . .'

Not that she is an authority on the subject of marriage, for her husband died within the year and she has never seen fit to seek another but has made a cult of widowhood.

Since the incident on Christmas day nobody has referred to mamma's extraordinary outburst, and all goes on as before. Mamma's recovery was short-lived, and from the beginning of the new year she has been confined to her room for most of the time and it is not safe for her to be left alone.

From the rock platform I cannot see the glen; the whole valley is filled with mist and even the waterfall vanishes less than halfway down its headlong plunge. But it is clear at the cove and I swim out into the calm limpid water which slips over my body like fluid silk. This is my true element; I should have been born a fish. At some distance from the shore I lie on my back and float. I have become much calmer in recent months so that I hardly ever experience one of my black moods. I am more responsive, more amenable, and father has commented favourably upon the change.

'You are settling down, Charles, and I am delighted to see it.'

But he is quite wrong. The truth is that I have learned to be more detached. I do what is expected of me but refuse to become involved. I am only deeply, hopelessly involved at one point, and he knows nothing of that.

And on that score I am greatly disturbed. Things have changed during my absence; Elizabeth has changed. She is as fond and delightful as ever, but there is a new reserve. Until now we have had few secrets and we have talked to each other with almost total freedom, now I sense that she is holding back. Sometimes she seems fearful that I shall touch on certain subjects and she becomes suddenly quite distant and uncharacteristically frivolous. I think and fear that I know the source of these changes. I have gathered from casual remarks of my father's and less casual remarks from aunt Florence that Gordon has been a more frequent visitor at the house while I have been away. He has been out riding with Elizabeth and once, chaperoned by aunt Florence, they went to a theatrical performance in Truro.

I refuse to believe that she feels more than a cousinly fondness for Gordon. The thought of her lithe, pale body . . . But I cannot bear to think such thoughts. I shall certainly have to talk to her soon, but I must wait until her birthday and the fête are over.

On my way back from the cove I find the park like an ant-hill with workmen everywhere. They are erecting a marquee on the lawn and suspending strings of lanterns and flags from the trees. One of the flatter fields on the east side of the house, part of the home farm, is given over to stalls and sideshows, swing-boats and roundabouts, while another is being pegged out for sports to suit all ages, from sack-racing to pitching the sheaf and bowling. There is to be a fortune-teller, a pretty girl from the gypsy encampment now in Job's Wood. She reminds me of Molly.

When I go down to breakfast father and aunt Florence are already seated, and Elizabeth's place is surrounded by little packages in brightly coloured wrappings. On one's birthday it is customary to be a little late for breakfast, then to look delightedly surprised at one's reception. My darling does it beautifully, her pleasure is so unaffected and natural. And she opens her packages in the right order. Papa and mamma, a string of pearls—her first item of real jewellery. Aunt Florence, a gold bangle with a snake's head. Uncle Arthur and aunt Amelia Jane, a cameo brooch which belonged to great-grandmother Clark. And from me, a cut-glass perfume spray with silver mountings. She looks from the thing to me in astonishment, and smiles. Aunt Florence's sharp eyes are estimating its value and father looks at me with a puzzled expression.

'Thank you—thank you all—such wonderful presents!'

There is one more package which she opens; it is a little book with gilt edges to the leaves. 'Look! Mr Ruskin's *Sesame and Lilies*, from Gordon. Isn't that kind of him?'

Gordon and Ruskin! I could laugh aloud if the idea was slightly less preposterous.

The fête begins at two o'clock. It is intended for the estate employees, our tenant farmers and workers, the villagers of St Martin and the people from the neighbouring hamlets, but there are always a few from as far afield as Tregony and Grampound—cuckoos in the nest who are liable to be very roughly handled by the locals. There are two bands, one on the lawn and the other on the sports field, and our guests tend to sort themselves into two groups; the better sort who are generally to be found in the park and the environs of the house, and the others who confine themselves to the two fields. The family is expected to circulate.

It is a glorious day, the hottest of the year so far. I see very little of Elizabeth, who is making herself agreeable to the women, whilst I have to interest myself in the activities of the men on the sports field. I catch sight of her talking to Gordon; Gordon, with a beard which he has been sedulously cultivating since I saw him in the spring. He wears a dark jacket and waistcoat with checked trousers, and looks passable. She is smiling up at him and I am bitterly jealous. I decide that I must find a moment to be alone with her, but I must not spoil her birthday.

From the lawn I glimpse mamma, dimly, through the window of her room, looking down at us. I wonder what she thinks about; is it possible that she feels as I do in one of my black moods but *all the time*? The thought makes me more sympathetic toward her, up there in her loneliness

Old Sandfield, the vicar, is trying to engage me in conversation about Oxford. I have the impression that the years he spent there were the only truly happy ones of his life. He questions me in minute detail about the survival of old customs to which he attaches great importance. What is the good of living to be sixty if all one's pleasant memories are of youth?

When I first became aware of Charles and began, in some strange way, to share his life, he was a quite separate person and I saw him and his family living lives of which I was only a spectator. This situation soon changed until I could not avoid identifying myself with him and I came to share his thoughts and his needs, to carry his responsibilities and experience his emotions. In every sense I became Charles Bottrell, but only in sporadic and unpredictable occurrences. These occurrences became more frequent and lasted longer until I seemed to be living his life with only occasional breaks in which I recovered my own identity. Those breaks, when I became myself once more, continued to the end but with one difference. Whereas previously, recovering my identity meant that I lost touch completely with Charles's world, it now happened that I sometimes found myself as Brian Kenyon, camping out in the squalid conditions I had created for myself in the old nursery, with the whole life of nineteenth century Tregear going on round me. I was like a prisoner looking through the window of his cell. These were the most bizarre experiences of all, and I think if they had been frequent or prolonged I might indeed have lost my reason.

My first experience of this kind came on the evening of the fête.

I had lost contact with Charles and was back in the old nursery, sitting in my chair in front of a smouldering fire which was almost choked by wood ash. To judge by the light it was evening. I lit the butane stove and put on some water to boil. From the remains of a tin of ham I cut a couple of slices, put them between bread and started to eat; the kettle began to sing and I reached for my jar of instant coffee. It was at this point that I became truly conscious of the commotion outside; I had been aware of it all along but now its significance came home to me. I went to the window and looked down. What I saw was the scene of which I had recently been part—as Charles Bottrell. People were milling about on the lawn; the strings of lanterns had been lowered and two men were lighting the candles inside. On the terrace, others were unpacking fireworks from boxes and arranging them for a display.

I looked down in utter amazement; it was Brian Kenyon who

was looking out of the window seeing these things, but what astonished and alarmed me was that I was seeing them, not from the nursery or day-room of Charles and Elizabeth, but from a bare dilapidated room in which there was a broken chair, a packing case and the other sordid evidence of my tramp-like existence.

I could see the neat, black-bearded figure of Joseph Bottrell as he stood talking to his loose-limbed, paunchy brother-in-law. Gordon was nearby with Elizabeth. She seemed unusually animated and they were laughing. Many of the people were strangers to me but Charles was there, looking worried and preoccupied, and I saw the vicar with his wife.

I felt excluded and resentful. I went to open the door but I could not grasp the door knob, my fingers would not close round it. I tried many times but the muscles of my hand refused to close in a grip sufficient to turn the knob. I went back to the window and in pointless exasperation banged on the glass with my knuckles, but no sound came, and I was not even aware of making contact with the glass. I was shut in! It was incredible! I tried to open the window but I was unable to exercise any purchase on the sash. It seemed that I was in a nightmare; helpless to make any impact on my surroundings and yet impelled urgently and desperately to do so.

There was a slight sound behind me and I turned with the nervous alertness of a trapped animal. Someone was opening the door, slowly and cautiously; a moment later Mary Bottrell, Charles's mother, stood there looking into the room, but it was obvious that she did not see me or, indeed, the room as I saw it. Her expression was strangely secretive, and after glancing round she turned away. I started forward but she closed the door before I could reach it, and when I grasped the knob it was unresponsive, as before. I listened as though my life depended on it and I heard her open the door of the next room. She must have gone in, for I heard her opening and closing drawers, then there was the sound of something being smashed—something of glass. There were other sounds which I could not identify, and then I heard no more.

It was difficult to explain why I was so frightened, why, after all my strange experiences, this particular one should have shared with my encounter in the maze an element of terror. Perhaps it was the same feeling of being trapped in some limbo between past and present and lacking the ability to make contact with either. My heart was racing and I was breathing rapidly, as though from great physical exertion. It seemed to me imperative that I should make contact with the world outside the room, and in desperation I picked up my saucepan with the intention of hurling it through the window, but my arms refused to obey me and the saucepan fell from my grasp.

At nine o'clock there is a firework display from the terrace. The lanterns are lit and everyone gathers on the lawn. It is one of those rare nights when the air is soft and warm like a caress against the skin. The first rocket shoots into the air and explodes in a shower of stars. There is a subdued exclamation of delight from the crowd. I find myself standing next to Elizabeth on the edge of the crowd, and I take her ungloved hand in mine.

'Happy birthday, darling.'

She squeezes my hand and I am happy.

By half-past nine it is all over, but it is after eleven before we get to bed. I am standing by the open window of my room, looking down into the yard. One of the horses is restless, snorting at intervals and pawing the ground. Parsons has just come in and there is a light in his room over the stables. There is a tap on my door and it opens immediately. Elizabeth is standing there, pale and tense.

'Charles!'

She beckons me and I follow her across the passage to her room. She opens a little drawer in her dressing table.

'I put my presents in there until I had a chance to look at them properly.'

The scent spray I gave her has been smashed into fragments and the silver mountings crushed almost beyond recognition; the gold bangle is a pathetic little lump of twisted metal and the cameo brooch looks at though it has been ground under someone's heel.

'The pearls?'

'They are scattered all over the floor. I keep standing on them.' Her voice trembles. 'It's not the presents, it's the hatred. What have I done?'

I take her in my arms, kiss her hair and murmur meaningless things; she sobs but she does not actually cry.

'Ah!'

Aunt Florence, who moves about the house in unnerving silence. She looks in the open drawer with no change of expression, then she turns to me. 'So your mother has been here.'

Perhaps I appear uncomprehending, for she goes on with some irritation: 'She is not in her room. God knows how long she has been out of it.'

'But how—?'

'That stupid maid looked in your mother's room just after ten o'clock and thought that she was asleep, so she went to bed herself. Fortunately I always check when I come upstairs, and I saw at once that your mother's bed had only been made to look as though there was someone in it.' After a moment she asks: 'Are you going to tell your father or shall I?'

'I will.'

'Very well. I shall organize a search of the house, but you had better tell your father that it is more likely that she is outside.'

'Outside?'

'The cloak and bonnet she wears for sitting out on the terrace are missing.'

She turns to the door and Elizabeth moves to follow.

'Where are you going?'

'To help you search.'

'You stay with your brother, or if you do not, lock yourself in your room.'

It is good advice, but I wish that it could have been given with greater kindness. We go downstairs together. Richards is in the hall and it is obvious that he has sensed something wrong.

'The master is in the drawing-room, Mr Charles.'

Father is sitting by the empty grate, smoking one of his slim cigars, a brandy glass on the table beside him. He looks up and it is clear that our appearance alarms him.

'Your mother?'

'She is not in her room and her cloak and bonnet are missing. Aunt Florence is organizing a search of the house.'

'Are you all right, Elizabeth?'

'Yes, papa.'

He comes toward her, full of concern. 'Are you quite sure, child?'

'Mamma has destroyed all her birthday presents.'

His distress is painful to see. He reaches out hesitantly and strokes her hair.

'My poor child! My poor, dear unfortunate child!'

There are tears in his eyes, the first I have ever seen there. I have always known how he loves Elizabeth, but he has never before allowed it to be so clearly seen.

'Look after your sister, Charles.'

The search of the house yields nothing, and the outdoor servants are roused from their beds for the thankless task of searching the grounds. If mamma is there and wishes to conceal herself there is little hope of finding her. Richards suggests that we use the three dogs which belong to the house, but father refuses quite brusquely. Apparently he feels that his refusal requires some explanation, for he turns to me:

'I will not have her hunted, Charles. She must not be made to feel in the slightest degree that she is a quarry.'

After a moment he asks: 'Shall you stay in the house with Elizabeth?'

I tell him that we intend to join in the search. He is about to protest but changes his mind. 'Do as you think best, but keep her with you, Charles.'

Parsons provides storm lanterns though there is little need, for the moon has risen and the sky is cloudless.

There is no proper system in the search, we keep running into others who are covering the same ground. Elizabeth and I have worked our way down through the park to the rock platform, exploring every one of the little-used paths which zigzag through the trees at different levels above the stream. Now we stand on the platform looking down at the maze and the pool. The pool is not directly in the moonlight, and except where it is churned into a bubbling cauldron by the fall its surface is dark.

Elizabeth shudders.

'No, you can put that out of your mind.'

'You think so?'

'I don't think that mamma has seriously attempted to kill herself.'

We start down the steep narrow path. To the left of the path there is a more or less sheer drop to the pool, to the right the rock rises vertically for a few feet, forming a wall, and some long-dead Bottrell excavated a grotto which he lined with shells. It has only a small entrance but inside is a large chamber, shaped like a beehive. At this point the path widens and we are able to walk side by side with me holding Elizabeth by the arm. I am about to look in the grotto for form's sake when a figure hurtles past me and grabs wildly at Elizabeth, so that I am almost dragged off balance in my effort to keep hold of her arm. For a few seconds it is touch and go whether we all three go over into the pool. Elizabeth's scream mingles with mamma's shriek, and is instantly followed by the splash as mamma's body hits the water. There is no possible doubt in my mind that she intended to take Elizabeth with her.

'Get help.'

Looking down I can see her cloak spread on the water like the wings of some great bird and her bonnet floating away. I remove my coat and boots and jump. It is not the first time I have done so, but never at night and with my clothes on. There is plenty of water, and when I surface I can see her struggling only five or six yards away, apparently entangled in her cloak.

I swim toward her and try to free her, but immediately I am involved in a nightmarish struggle. She grabs my arms so that her nails sink into my flesh and I am amazed by her strength. We go under together and surface again. She must have swallowed a good deal of water, but her struggles become if anything more violent and her grip on my arms does not relax for an instant. I know that there is shallow water only a few yards off and I strike out in that direction, swimming with my legs, but the drag of her clothing is too much for me. We sink at least twice more, and I am beginning to weaken. By a tremendous effort I manage to free one arm, but she at once grabs my hair and pulls my head under. This is so unexpected and so deliberate that I am totally unprepared and I swallow a lot of water. I am aware of pressure in my head, of heaviness in my lungs and roaring in my ears.

It dawns on me that in her madness she is mistaking me for Elizabeth and that she is deliberately trying to drown me; it is my last coherent thought for some time. Now it is I who struggle— to free myself, certainly, but to achieve something else? I do not know. I am filled with hatred for this woman who is my mother, who has twice tried to murder my sister. My frenzy matches hers.

It does not last much longer; she goes limp, there are two or three convulsive spasms and then she is still. With what strength I have left I swim for the shallow water, towing her after me. When help arrives I am sitting on the bank and she is lying beside me, her feet still in the water.

CHAPTER TEN

CHARLES WAS NEVER more than dimly aware of that other who seemed to exist at the very limits of his perception, like someone who hovers on the fringes of memory, always eluding total recall. Since the strange episode in the maze the *other* had seemed vaguely benevolent and he was conscious of a mysterious and growing rapport, but he could know nothing of the life and times of Brian Kenyon.

It was a one-sided relationship. As Brian Kenyon I had intimate knowledge of what it was like to think and feel and be Charles Bottrell. More than that, I knew that he was drawing rapidly nearer to an even greater crisis in his life which would, in some unknown way, remove him from his family so that they would never hear of him again and never know the time or manner of his death. As I had become more deeply involved with Charles, as I had committed my personality more completely to his, it seemed increasingly necessary to try to break through the barrier, to reach him as Brian Kenyon and even to warn him of what lay ahead. I think that it was my effort to do this which was responsible for the 'limbo' experiences I have described, when I was unable to establish real contact with either past or present yet remained aware of both. Perhaps my frustration was a measure of the impossibility of that task.

Immediately after Charles's ordeal I lost contact; I was excluded again at the very moment when I would have given so much to be with him, to *be* him. From my prison in the old nursery I could watch and listen. I saw two of the estate men carrying Mary Bottrell's body on a hurdle and Joseph walking behind, as in a few days he would follow the bier at her funeral. Charles had come back half-an-hour before, wrapped in somebody's cloak. He was unsteady on his legs but he had obviously refused help from Blight, who walked beside him. Elizabeth was in her room next door and I fancied that from time to time I could hear voices.

This was the night of Saturday 20th June 1868, and I recalled the article in the local paper which I had read on my first visit: 'On June 20th 1868 Mary Anne died after an illness which had lasted several years . . .'

The words had meant nothing to me at the time, now I had lived through the last frenzied moments of her life. For me she was no longer just a name on the family vault, she was that strange, obsessed creature with slightly bulging eyes who one night, after attempting to stab her daughter, had tried desperately to bridge the gulf which separated her from her son. 'On the lips, Charles . . . on the lips . . . Do I revolt you, Charles? . . . I am thirty-seven, that's all—not an *old* woman.' Now she was dead.

'. . . and a month later, still in deep mourning for her mother, Elizabeth married her cousin, Gordon Clark, who was employed in her father's bank.'

The account in the newspaper by some local historian had become for me the programme of events, a schedule, but there was nothing I could do. I sat in my chair and listened to the continuing commotion around me, and by the time the house had recovered its peace there was light in the sky and sunrise was not far off.

My mother is to be buried this afternoon after an inquest in which the coroner found that she had accidentally drowned. He expressed great sympathy with the family, was very respectful to my father and kindly to me. I played my hypocritical rôle to perfection. It was easy, for this subdued, muted proceeding had nothing to do with those moments of wild demoniac madness in which my mother met her death.

Father follows the coffin with aunt Florence; Elizabeth and I walk behind. Elizabeth is covered from head to foot in black and I can see only the pale outline of her face through a veil of black lace. At the graveside I am next to her, holding her arm, while on the other side of the grave Gordon stands with his family, and from time to time he raises his eyes to look across at Elizabeth.

Elizabeth and I have had very little to say to each other since Saturday. I think that we have avoided being alone together, perhaps because we both realise that we are nearing a watershed in our relationship.

After the funeral the mourners return to the house and they are plied with food and drink. As I watch and listen to them going through the prescribed ritual for the occasion I try to think what my mother's death means to me. I want to feel something but I do not succeed. For a short time there was this lovely creature who, at intervals, visited the nursery, swept me off my feet and smothered me with kisses, then left, leaving behind a lingering, cloying perfume. This exotic being vanished, and in her place there was a sombre woman who seemed to brood over the whole house and hold us all to ransom with her lightning changes of mood, her suspicious eyes, her secretive smile and her sarcastic, grating laugh; the woman who hated and tried to kill my sister. It is she who has died and I feel nothing; no remorse, no regret, not even a sense of relief.

I have been lying in bed only a short time when Elizabeth comes in, in her dressing gown. She speaks softly.

'Are you asleep?'

'No.'

'I must talk to you, Charles.'

'About mother?'

'No.'

'I'll light the lamp.'

'No! Let us talk as we are.'

She sits on the edge of my bed, and it is not light enough for me to see more than the pale oval of her face. I take her hand, which is cold.

'I am going to have a baby, Charles.'

It is as though my stomach suddenly contracts in a spasm of nausea. 'But that is impossible, Elizabeth! You can't have a baby unless—.'

She makes a movement of impatience. 'Don't treat me like a fool,

Charles! I'm going to have a baby, I'm *pregnant,* do you understand?'

Pregnant! I detest the very word with all its associations, and that it should be linked with Elizabeth revolts me. It is as though she has confided that she is suffering from some loathsome disease.

Without meaning to do so I withdraw my hand from hers.

'Are you quite sure? Isn't it easy to be mistaken?'

Her voice is flat and toneless. 'There is no mistake, Charles, I am quite certain.'

'Have you told anyone?'

'No.'

She sits there, a small white figure, and I am ashamed of my fastidious cowardice. 'Who is it?'

She does not answer, and despite myself my voice acquires an edge of impatience: 'Who is it, Elizabeth?'

'Gordon.'

'I'll kill him!'

She sighs as an adult might do over a child's foolishness. 'For God's sake, Charles! Gordon did no more than I encouraged him to do.'

'Does he know?'

She does not answer and there is silence between us. I am torn by hatred and love, jealousy and tenderness.

'Have you decided what you shall do?'

'We shall marry, of course. What else?' She sounds so coldly matter-of-fact that I could weep.

'That is out of the question!'

She is on the defensive at once. 'Why is it out of the question?'

'For one thing you don't love him.'

She gets up and goes to the window, where she stands looking out at the vague outline of the stable block. 'Is it likely that I shall love anyone I marry? Would you wish me to?'

I am silent.

'You are a romantic, Charles, and I have shocked you.'

'I cannot understand how you could allow Gordon to—.'

She turns quickly, almost fiercely. 'Don't say it, Charles! I know of your visits to Molly Couch, and of the affair with the Kenyon girl.'

I am robbed of words. These things have never been discussed between us and I cannot imagine how she came by her knowledge, but there is, clearly, a great deal which I do not understand.

She sits once more on my bed and takes my hand. 'Is Molly Couch disgusted by what you do, Charles? Does she let you only for the money?'

'But Elizabeth—.'

'Answer me, Charles!'

'She is not disgusted and she does not do it for the money.'

'Is she passionate?'

'Yes, but—.'

'And the Kenyon girl, did you rape her?'

I am deeply shocked at these questions. 'No!'

'Don't let us quarrel, Charles. You and I are too much alike, we are two of a kind; sometimes I think that we are in love with our own reflections. The difference is that, as a man, you have your freedom; as a woman, marrying Gordon is as near as I shall ever get to having mine.'

'You call marriage to Gordon freedom?'

Her manner is defiant. 'Yes, I do. Gordon and I understand each other, we shall come to terms. For once, Charles, try to see things from my point of view.'

I do not really understand what she is talking about but, oddly, Molly comes into my mind, lying naked at my side after making love.

'Aren't you afraid that I shall give you another baby?'

'What of it? If you don't he will. As long as the poor little bastard has black hair it don't signify.'

Marriage has given Molly a kind of freedom. And it was she who said, 'I reckon a woman 'as to be woke up, so to speak, and some sleep sounder 'n others.'

The moon has risen and it is now light enough for me to see Elizabeth's face clearly. She is looking at me with a thoughtful expression and I am surprised that she does not appear more distressed.

'Charles you remember the day at Kiberick when you asked me to take my clothes off?'

'Of course I remember.'

'I told you not to touch me but I wanted you to take me in your arms.'

I am deeply moved but also troubled by her words.

'If you had done so, you might have been the father of my baby.'

Guilty thoughts which have troubled the darkest recesses of my mind, forbidden images which I have rigorously suppressed as too monstrous for a moment's scrutiny are brought into the light of day and clothed in words. By my sister.

I dare not travel further along that path, and take refuge in being practical.

'What can I do?'

She squeezes my hand. 'Nothing, Charles; just be patient with me.'

'How long is it?'

She hesitates for a moment, then says, 'Long enough.'

For a rare moment I am thinking not of Elizabeth, or of myself, but of our poor father.

'Will you let me tell father?'

'Why should you tell him?'

'Because he may say things which he will afterwards regret.'

She ruffles my hair. 'Sometimes I feel a great deal older than you, brother Charles.'

'But you agree?'

'Of course not!'

It was morning and I woke, knowing that I was no longer confined. I saw my sleeping bag and the packing case, my chair and the ash-filled grate, my few utensils and meagre stock of food. I knew that all round me there were empty rooms, that if I turned the knob of the door it would open on to a bare, deserted corridor.

I got up and was surprised to find myself weak. I had a headache, as though from a hangover. The day was overcast with drizzling rain and the room was cold. I raked out the fireplace, filling the air with fine dust, relaid the fire and lit it. I washed and shaved carefully as I had not done for some time—I cannot say how long—and afterwards I made myself some breakfast, a boiled egg with a crust of very stale bread. I felt as though I was convalescent after a long illness.

When I had eaten I wandered about the house in an aimless fashion and finally I went out into the yard, to the coach house, where I stood for a while looking at the Mini as though it were something totally unfamiliar. It occurred to me that I could get into the car and in less than half-an-hour I could be at my digs where Clarice would be only too pleased to fuss over me. I could return to school, and after a few half-hearted enquiries and, perhaps, an official rebuke everything would be as it had been before. It was a pipe-dream.

It is Saturday morning and we are at breakfast. The room is utterly silent except when someone replaces a cup in its saucer or a knife on a plate. Outside the sun shines and there is every promise of another hot day. Elizabeth, in her black silk mourning dress, sits bolt upright, looking straight before her. She is even paler than usual and her eyes are surrounded by unaccustomed puffiness. There are no servants in the room for it is the custom for us to serve ourselves at breakfast. Aunt Florence wears a set expression, like a mask. My father eats mechanically and keeps his eyes lowered. He too is very pale, and there are tell-tale rings of sleeplessness round his eyes. Since the conventional greetings and grace no word has been spoken. It seems that the room is suspended in space, isolated from any possible contact with the outside.

My father clears his throat. 'I have sent Parsons with the carriage to fetch Gordon and his parents.' He looks at us each in turn as though seeking acknowledgement or even approval, but none of us gives any sign. 'When they arrive I will talk to them in the library and I shall be grateful if you will, all three, be available in the drawing-room. This is a family matter, concerning us all.'

The silence returns and becomes almost palpable.

Aunt Florence arranges her knife and fork on her plate with meticulous care. 'Do you wish me to receive them when they come, Joseph?'

My father shakes his head. 'No, Florence, thank you. I have asked Richards to bring them to the library.'

Elizabeth has given him the news but I have not heard what passed between them. When I saw her afterwards she was distressed but all she said was: 'He wept, Charles.'

'Was he not angry?'

'No, but please do not ask me about it now.'

Father glances round the table to satisfy himself that we have all finished, then he tinkles the little silver bell beside his plate to summon the servants. The three of us cross the hall to the drawing-room while he goes toward the library.

Aunt Florence takes her customary seat by the window and picks up her embroidery. Elizabeth takes a copy of the *Illustrated London News* from a side table and sits down with the paper in her lap. At a loss what to do or say, I stand by the fireplace. In a few minutes we hear the carriage wheels on the gravel and see it pass the window. There are voices in the hall as they are greeted by Richards. I wonder if they have any idea why they have been summoned. The brief commotion in the hall is over, the library door closes and we settle down to wait.

Aunt Florence is the first to speak.

'You did not choose to confide in me, Elizabeth.'

Elizabeth answers calmly, 'No, aunt Florence.'

Four or five more stitches go into the embroidery before aunt Florence speaks again.

'Had you done so I might have persuaded you to another course.'

'Another course, aunt?'

Elizabeth's apparent calm disturbs me, it seems fragile, brittle.

'At least to consider an alternative to hasty marriage which, in all the circumstances, cannot fail to be a great embarrassment to the family and damaging to your poor papa.'

'What alternative, aunt?'

Aunt Florence turns her cold eyes on me. 'I would rather have discussed this with you woman to woman but I am prevented from doing so. However, my suggestion would have been that you should go away for a time—a visit, perhaps, to France. Other young girls of your class, faced with your difficulty, have solved it in this manner. They return in due time and no one is the wiser or the worse.'

'And the child?'

Aunt Florence frowns. 'Is adopted, of course.' She adds after a moment: 'It is still not too late to speak to your father of the possibility. I will gladly do so on your behalf.'

Elizabeth is icily calm. 'There would be no point.'

In the silence which follows I try to imagine what is happening in the next room. After the first shock and expressions of incredulity, my father will have to face the pompous absurdities of uncle Arthur and the colourful indiscretions of aunt Amelia Jane. And from Gordon? How is he reacting? My imagination will not carry me that far; I am beginning to think that I have underestimated him. If he is a buffoon he is a dangerous buffoon.

There is movement in the hall and a little later Richards comes in.

'The master wishes to see you in the library, Miss Elizabeth.'

Elizabeth gets up, glances at me and goes out.

Aunt Florence, so agitated that she is unable to concentrate on her embroidery, puts it aside.

'Parsons is waiting for them with the carriage.'

I say nothing and the silence lengthens. The embroidery has been a sort of barrier, now it is gone. We are facing each other like two wrestlers.

'Your father will destroy himself for you ungrateful children!'

I still say nothing and my silence exasperates her.

'It . . . it *disgusts* me, and I blame you for most of it!'

She hesitates for a moment or two longer, then stands up. 'I cannot bear to be here in the room with you; I shall go upstairs, and if your father wishes to see me he can send for me.'

She goes out, closing the door behind her.

I am alone. Everything seems unreal, the sunshine outside, the room, aunt Florence, Elizabeth, father, me . . . it is as though we are all acting in a play of which the end has not been written.

I have no idea how long I stand staring out of the window, but at last there is movement. There is subdued conversation in the hall, then I hear my father's voice outside and I move away from the window to avoid being seen. A moment or two later father comes into the room.

'Your aunt is not here?'

'She has gone to her room.'

He walks to the window and stands with his back to me.

'You have a right to know what has been decided, Charles.'

I say nothing.

'Elizabeth will be married on July 20th, that is to say, in a little over three weeks. Obviously it will be a very quiet wedding —a family occasion only, for we are still in mourning.'

He is irritated by my silence, which is not deliberate.

'It is the best solution, Charles—it is the only possible solution consistent with morality, and it is what Elizabeth wants.'

His voice falters and I feel moved, but I am incapable of making any response which would betray my emotion.

'For the time being they will live at Danzig House; that will be conveniently near the bank for Gordon. I shall arrange a marriage settlement and I propose to increase Gordon's emolument at the bank—something which, in justice, I should have done anyway in the near future, for he is proving a valuable young man.'

After a brief pause, during which he waits for some sign from me, he goes on: 'I know that you do not like him, Charles. I also know how fond you are of your sister, but, believe me, a woman who finds a kind and considerate partner is likely to enjoy a greater share of continuing happiness than one who enters upon a relationship which is more passionate and, therefore, more demanding.'

It seems an odd remark in the circumstances, and I am startled by his apparent insight. I try to think of something to say which will meet him halfway, but fail.

'None of this will affect your inheritance, Charles, or your ultimate position in the bank.'

'I am not concerned about those things, father.'

He turns to face me for the first time. 'No, Charles, I know. I wish that you were.'

I suppose that this will end our conversation, but he has more to say.

'Elizabeth is a remarkable young woman, Charles, with great

strength of character.' He pauses for some time as though carefully choosing his words. 'I do not, of course, condone what has happened; what I am saying is that she will overcome her difficulties and make a success of her marriage if she is allowed to.'

What he says could be true.

I am at sea.

CHAPTER ELEVEN

DURING THE LAST phase of Charles's life at Tregear I was identified with him for long periods, and the intervals during which I recovered my own personality were short and confused so that I recall them as one remembers a night of troubled dreams. This does not mean that my experience of his life had become continuous, it remained a series of flashbacks, but each one might cover the events of a whole day or more than a day. There was never any obvious connection between time for Brian Kenyon and time for Charles Bottrell. Although, camping out as I was, I lost count of the days, it is obvious in retrospect that the events I lived through in Charles's life did not occupy a corresponding length of time in my own.

My emotions were now so completely involved with Charles and his sister that the approaching crisis, in which it seemed Charles might lose his life, affected me profoundly. The succession of events which culminated in his disappearance was imprinted on my mind with the clarity of a visible calendar. Mary Anne Bottrell was buried on 24th June; Elizabeth was due to marry her cousin on 20th July and five days later Charles would leave home, never to be seen again. I was convinced that Charles had died at that time and so, it seemed, I was faced with an impending tragedy. I could not see it as an event in the past but the fact that it was inevitable only made it more terrible. My feelings for Charles were stronger and deeper than any I have known, and I can imagine that they were comparable with the bond which sometimes exists between identical twins. Not knowing to what extent I should be permitted to share in his last days added to my distress, and I was torn between a desire to experience all that he experienced and a natural dread of the event itself.

What I came to look upon as the last act began one evening when I was walking aimlessly in the park. Suddenly it seemed that the air grew warmer and the sky lighter; for an instant everything about me dissolved into a hazy blur as if my eyes had lost their focus, and I experienced a moment of complete mental confusion. These, with minor variations, were the symptoms of transition which I now recognized, and then, abruptly, I am Charles Bottrell, with no knowledge or memory of having been anyone else.

Sunday evening. The bells of St Martin's pealing for Evensong. The peal ends and the tenor bell starts 'tolling in'.

Father will be there at the end of the family pew, aunt Florence next to him and Elizabeth on the inside. In the pew behind the Clarks in strength, all in full mourning. The family does not always attend Evensong but this is a gesture, a showing of the flag in which I have refused to take part. Instead, here I am, wandering aimlessly.

On this warm, sunny evening the west door will remain open throughout the service, and at some point the low sun will shine straight down the aisle, lighting up the altar where, in sixteen hours from now, Elizabeth will marry her bucolic cousin.

'Elizabeth Mary, wilt thou have this man to be thy wedded husband . . .?'

'I will, for I have his child inside me.'

Last night I had a strange dream. I was in the passage outside my bedroom when the clock on the landing was striking midnight. I remember counting the strokes as one sometimes does, and when I had reached twelve I assumed that there would be no more but the strokes continued, punctuating the rest of my dream. From the passage I entered the old nursery and I was astonished to see that the room was empty—empty, that is, of all our furniture, books, pictures, carpet and curtains. The walls were peeling and the floor was bare boards. There was a very large wooden box, an old chair and other things which I cannot remember.

My friend, my *alter ego* of the maze, was there, sitting in the old broken chair, and he was using the wooden box as a table. It was night and he was reading with the aid of a lamp which gave off such a brilliant light that my eyes were dazzled if I looked at it directly. I was standing behind his chair yet he seemed unaware of me. It was a strange sensation. On the box there were several books and papers, some of which I recognized as belonging to my father, and there were some notes which it seemed that my friend had written himself. The handwriting was curiously cramped, but I deciphered my own name and some reference to Elizabeth.

I felt drawn toward him and I reached out to touch him on the shoulder. In my dream my fingers made contact with the material of his jacket. He turned to look at me and, as in the maze, the face I saw was almost though not quite my own. He was smiling, a gentle smile, full of understanding, and his lips moved, but in the perverse manner of dreams I could not hear what it was that he said. I became aware of the great effort he was making to bridge the gap between us, and I responded with all the concentration of which I was capable, but at that moment the clock on the stairs stopped striking and I woke, feeling cheated.

I chose not to go to church with the family and now here I am, at a loss how to spend my time. I come out into the cove and walk past the cottages. Molly is at her door as usual and a barely perceptible sign passes between us.

'Good evening, Molly.'

'Good evening, Mr Charles.'

I have not been near her since my mother's funeral and I wondered what sort of reception I should get, but all seems to be well.

I need her.

Although it is Sunday I know that the boats will set out by ten o'clock. Times are too hard for the fishermen to observe the old tradition of waiting until midnight on the Sabbath. I walk on across the beach where the men are preparing for sea.

Since the funeral I have seen little of Elizabeth. Preparations for the wedding and after have gone on almost surreptitiously, and I have been told very little; most of what I know I have learned by inference. There is to be no honeymoon because we are still in mourning, and in any case it is considered unwise for Elizabeth to travel far from home. There has been vague talk of an extended holiday after the birth of the baby.

Elizabeth spends most of her time in Truro, supervising the making ready of Danzig House. I have not seen much of Gordon, but when we meet I am, at Elizabeth's urgent request, civil, though I cannot find it in my heart even to counterfeit friendship. I spend most of my time drifting aimlessly about, immersed in a tepid bath of nostalgia, which is absurd, for there has been little in my life which I can look back on with much pleasure. This summer evening chimes in well with my mood; the calm sea, the golden light, the stillness and the sweetness which cloys. I wish that I could die as effortlessly as the day.

I think of Molly and my heart warms to her blatant vulgarity.

I stay out on the cliffs in the gathering darkness until I see the boats put to sea, then I make for the cottage.

Molly says: 'So Miss Elizabeth is getting wed.'

'Yes.'

'Quick enough.'

I say nothing.

'I mean after the mistress dying like that.'

'It's no business of yours.'

'No. Sorry, I'm sure.'

And a little later: 'You'll miss her, I reckon.'

'What are you saying now?'

'Nothing, but I've always thought you two was closer than most brothers an' sisters.'

I look down at her dark, wild eyes. 'You're a witch, Molly; a foul-mouthed, dirty witch, but I love you.'

She laughs. 'That'll be the day. My mother told me never to trust a man's words when he's drinking or screwing.'

I leave her just after midnight and walk up through the park. I let myself in by the kitchen door into the yeasty, oppressive warmth, cross the hall, climb the stairs and go to my own room.

Ten minutes after I am in bed Elizabeth comes in in her nightgown.

'I've been waiting for you to come back.'

She sits on the bed beside me and I reach for her hand.

'You've been with her?'

'Yes.'

'Oh, Charles!'

She pulls back the bedclothes and slips in beside me. 'Hold me, Charles . . . Hold me!' Her lips find mine. 'Do I kiss like her, Charles? *Do* I?' Her body arches against mine and her hands clutch at my back, kneading the flesh through my shirt. 'Hold me tighter, Charles . . . tighter! Hurt me, my love.' She speaks in harsh, demanding whispers. 'You must teach me, Charles . . .'

She releases me abruptly and sits up.

'What are you doing?'

She pulls off her nightgown over her head. 'Now you shall have me as I was on the beach.'

Naked, she leans over me, her warm sweet breath on my face. 'What does it matter now? Don't you see? . . . Love me, Charles . . . I want you to . . . Kiss my breasts . . . This is our night, dearest . . . You must love me . . .'

I am drawn deeper and deeper into a vortex, my mind skirts the fringes of oblivion; I am blind but my senses tell of a beating heart, of velvet warmth and honeyed sweetness. I am held a willing prisoner long after my passion is spent.

*

She walks up the aisle on my father's arm followed by Priscilla, her only bridesmaid. I cannot believe that this serene, immaculate being has been my lover. Her jet black hair showing through her veil and the red roses of her bouquet are all that there is to relieve the whiteness of her gown.

I am profoundly troubled and confused. I have grown up with the idea that it is I who lead and she who follows; it seemed in the natural order of things. It has been her role to restrain my excesses, to stand for the conventions, to be the conscience of us both. But it is for me to set the pattern and the pace, and only I am privileged to be outrageous.

Gordon is at the altar, an ungainly figure in black, and she stands by his side. She lifts her veil.

'Dearly beloved, we are gathered together here in the sight of

God, and in the face of this congregation . . .' Sandfield begins to weave his spell.

Elizabeth has always furnished unwavering standards by which I might choose to judge myself, and through her I could be encouraged, cajoled, persuaded and gently scolded into a sufficient conformity. She was submissive, admiring, loving and forbearing.

'I require and charge you both, as ye shall answer at the dreadful day of judgement when the secrets of all hearts shall be disclosed, that if either of you know any impediment . . .'

But that Elizabeth has vanished in the night, and in her place is the girl who lay naked in my bed, her lovely features contorted and her body ravished in the act of love; that same girl who now stands at the altar pledging herself to a man she cannot love.

'Elizabeth Mary, wilt thou have this man to thy wedded husband to live together after God's ordinance in the holy estate of matrimony . . .?'

Her voice is firm and clear. 'I will.'

Afterwards the bridal bouquet is placed with the withered flowers on the family vault. There is a man with a photographic apparatus to make a picture of bride and groom outside the church. All the women of the village are there.

Back at the house the reception is on a very small scale with only relatives and close friends. For me, the rest of the day passes in a daze. I suppose that I behave normally for no one suggests otherwise, but I seem to blunder through an unfamiliar world. Gordon is gracious to everybody and especially to me. At one stage, when I can stand it no longer, I go out on to the terrace and he follows me. He is red-faced from too much wine.

'I am a very lucky man, Charles. I know how close you and Elizabeth are . . .'

The fool knows nothing.

'I shall never seek to take your place, Charles, either with Elizabeth or in your father's business . . .'

Perhaps he feels that he is not expressing himself very tactfully, for he breaks off and tries again.

'Some day we shall have to work together and I think that we should bear this in mind.'

In deference to his improved fortune he now wears gold instead of steel-rimmed spectacles, but his appearance is no less owl-like.

'You are looking ahead again, Gordon—making plans.'

He laughs nervously. 'You are your father's son, Charles, you can afford to live in the present. That is really what I am trying to say—I know that the bank's affairs do not interest you, and in the years to come you will need someone who has been brought up in the business to look after things. Of course, all this is a long way off, but it is possible that we could come to an arrangement which would be to our mutual advantage, don't you think?'

I say nothing because I can think of nothing to say. He looks at me, obviously wondering whether he has blundered.

'I feel that I owe the family a great deal, Charles.'

'Do you, Gordon?'

They are to spend the night at Tregear and move to Truro in the morning.

The day ends at last, but I cannot stay in the house while they go to bed so I go walking on the cliffs. It is another balmy night with scarcely a ripple on the water, but I am plagued by imaginings.

I had whispered: 'Tomorrow night it will be your husband.'

And she had answered with complete casualness: 'No; I shall be indisposed.'

But will he be so gently submissive now that he is in possession?

It has always been on the sea that I have found my greatest pleasure in life—swimming and sailing. It is there that I have come nearest to self-forgetfulness. At such times the little red-eyed, sharp toothed rodent, the real me, can become a somnolent pussy cat who purrs when stroked.

They say that a good swimmer cannot drown himself. I wonder!

I meet them at breakfast. Father is going to the bank as usual and bride and groom will travel with him in the carriage to their new home. Early this morning one of the farm carts set out with the last of Elizabeth's belongings, and the thought brings me near to tears.

Gordon comes down before Elizabeth and stands, awkward and humble, waiting until father waves him to his seat. After the initial greeting he sits silently, staring down at the table.

'Another very pleasant day,' father remarks.

'Yes, sir, it is—very pleasant.'

Father wants to put him at his ease. 'As you know, Gordon, I shall be leaving for Tavistock later this morning.' He turns to me, trying to engage us both in conversation. 'You see, Charles, the bank has an indirect interest in Devon Great Consols, and what with the falling price of copper and continuing labour unrest in the mines, we are becoming concerned. I shall meet some of the adventurers and try to discover what the prospects are.' He pauses for some comment, and when none comes, he adds: 'I shall return on Friday.'

Elizabeth comes in. What I expected I do not know, but I am astonished to see her looking just as usual. She takes her place, smiling across at me. 'I apologise for being late, papa. Aunt Florence has a headache and asked me to tell you that she will not be down.'

'Ah! What a pity, on your last morning.' He rings the bell and the servants bring in dishes which they place on the sideboard for us to serve ourselves.

'I was saying, Elizabeth, I shall be away until Friday, but I hope that you and Gordon will spend Saturday and Sunday at Tregear.'

'I am sure that we shall both want to do that, papa.'

'Danzig House is well enough for the present, but we must find you a house on the hill above the town,' father says. 'I am quite sure that the low-lying parts of Truro are not conducive to good health. Don't you agree, Gordon?'

'I am sure that you are right, sir.'

All this so that the yokel may continue to force his attentions on my sister in the security of the marriage bed.

They are leaving. Elizabeth throws her arms round my neck and kisses me. 'You will come to see me, Charles?' She does not say 'us'.

'Of course.'

158

'Often?'

'Often.'

'That is a promise!'

They drive off, my father with his back to the coachman, the two of them facing him.

Tregear is empty and desolate.

*

I was in the maze, standing by the stone table with its enigmatic inscription. It was a sunny April morning—warm, and sweet with the scents of spring. I could hear the waterfall, subdued yet remorseless, underscoring the staccato screech of the circular saw as it sliced through bough after bough. Events were moving towards a climax, but I was still under the influence of Charles's mood of confusion and distress as he began to grasp the implications of Elizabeth's marriage. It seemed to him that in achieving unsought the fulfilment of his love he had destroyed its object, and that nothing remained but the prospect of a sordid intrigue.

I recalled Amelia's commonplace book and her distress on reading her mother's testament. 'In case of my death to be handed to Amelia when she reaches mature age.' What secret had Elizabeth to confide to her daughter other than the knowledge of the girl's true parentage? Arthur Clark believed that Amelia's preoccupation with outbreeding arose from her concern at being the child of a marriage between first cousins, in a family with a background of insanity. How much greater her justification had she known herself to be the offspring of a truly incestuous relationship!

I threaded my way through the maze and climbed the slope to the rock platform. There were still unanswered questions, but a pattern was beginning to emerge.

I made my way through the overgrown shrubbery and came out in sight of the house, which looked shabby and neglected in the revealing sunlight. For me it was no impersonal remnant of times past, it enshrined part of my life as surely as if I had been born Charles Joseph Bottrell.

I entered the house through the plank door, which I had not locked, and went upstairs to the nursery. On my packing-case table there was a cardboard box of groceries with cans of beer on the top and a note:

'In case you are still interested, it is Saturday again—a week since I was here last. If you died of starvation it would be on my conscience, otherwise I don't care a damn.

'For God's sake wash your socks or something.

'K.'

I went out into the corridor and shouted her name, then I went down to the stable yard to see if her car was there but she had left. I have to admit that I was not sorry.

I was still standing in the yard when I began to experience once more the symptoms of transition—the loss of focus in my eyes, the mental confusion and a sense of giddiness.

Wilkes has saddled the mare and is holding her head for me to mount.

'Thank you, Wilkes. I shall be back early this evening.'

It is Thursday, two days since Elizabeth drove off with her husband to the house in Truro, and I have decided to visit her for the simple reason that I can no longer remain in suspense.

I ride briskly into Truro, leave my horse in the Red Lion stables, and have luncheon in the hotel dining-room. Afterwards I present myself at Danzig House. The door is answered by a pretty parlour-maid who is new to me, but as soon as she hears my name she says: 'The mistress gave instructions that if you came you was to go up at once, sir.'

'Where is she?'

'In her boudoir, sir. The room at the end of the passage.'

So madam has a boudoir.

I go upstairs to a room in the end of the house which was once a bedroom. It overlooks a small garden and catches the afternoon sun. Elizabeth, wearing a loose wrap, is working on a watercolour on an easel placed in the window.

'Charles!'

She drops her brush and has her arms round me, smothering me with kisses.

'I thought that you would never come!'

She sits on the sofa and pats the cushion beside her. 'Sit close to me, Charles, I want to feel you near me.'

She is still my black-haired, white-skinned, adorable sister.

When our flood of chatter has run dry, we sit gazing at each other and holding hands. After a moment she says: 'Nothing has changed for us, Charles; we are as we were.'

I am taken on a conducted tour of the house and I am astonished by the changes she has made in so short a time. With no structural alterations, and using most of the existing furniture, she has contrived by a skilful use of new hangings and covers to give the old house an appearance of freshness and charm which I would not have believed possible.

Back in her room, she pulls the bell rope. 'We will take tea, Charles.'

And we do, from a Royal Worcester service which was a wedding present from father. I cannot make up my mind whether her obvious pleasure is in the novelty of playing hostess, or in my company, or whether it has deeper roots. Certainly I have never seen her happier or more beautiful.

'Marriage seems to agree with you.'

She looks at me with a curious expression, faintly amused, perhaps a little puzzled. Then she says with great seriousness: 'Gordon and I each have exactly what we wanted. Why should we not be happy?'

'I refuse to believe that you wanted Gordon.'

She reaches out and squeezes my hand. 'You are stupid, Charles!'

I say, at last, that it is time for me to go and she does not try to dissuade me, but she hugs me warmly and makes me promise to come often and earlier.

'*Much* earlier, Charles—we can spend whole days together. There is nothing which we may not do.'

The pretty parlourmaid shows me out and I find myself walking along Quay Street confused and ill at ease. There are questions which I dare not ask. With all her warmth and with all her love, Elizabeth is manoeuvring me into playing a part in which I am expected to understand a great deal more than I do.

It is early on a golden summer evening, and I walk for the sake of walking. At the top of Pydar Street I turn off toward Kenwyn and then down the hill to the stream. I follow the stream as far up as Idless, cross over and return by a footpath along the leat to Moresk Mill on the outskirts of the town. The walk has taken me longer than I had supposed, for it is already dusk. I arrive at the foot of Goodwives' Lane; the narrow, steeply sloping street is deserted, but as I start to climb the hill a man comes out of one of the houses some distance ahead. He looks round with obvious nervousness, then hurries off up the hill. The figure is unmistakable, it is Gordon. I wonder what business has brought him to this part of town, which is barren ground for bankers. Then I remember my father's words: '. . . a house in Goodwives' Lane run by a Mrs Kilthorpe; she is discreet . . .'

I reach the house, which is considerably larger and in much better shape than its neighbours. The entrance is down a narrow alley, and on the spur of the moment I go down the alley and knock on the door. I want to be quite sure.

The door is opened almost at once by a respectably dressed middle-aged woman.

'Mrs Kilthorpe?'

'Yes. What can I do for you?'

'I have been recommended by Mr Clark.'

'Recommended?'

'I think you know what I mean.'

'You are a friend of Mr Clark?'

'His brother-in-law.'

'You will need to make an appointment.'

I make some excuse and leave. I collect my horse from the stables and ride back at a leisurely pace through the darkness. I hand over my horse to the boy and go into the house. Aunt Florence has the most acute hearing, and she is waiting for me in the hall.

'It would be a convenience for the servants, Charles, if you would leave word when you intend to return.'

I say nothing and go upstairs to my room. Elizabeth's words repeat themselves endlessly in my mind:

'Gordon and I each have exactly what we wanted. Why should we not be happy?'

*

I was in a sorry state with no idea what was happening to me. I had lost all sense of time and I was no longer capable of any sustained effort. I sat in my chair in the old nursery with no inclination to do anything else. I had no clear recollection of when I had last eaten or of when I had had proper sleep, though I frequently dozed in my chair. The grate was once more choked with ash, and it sometimes seemed to me that the room was very cold. Occasionally there was rain on the window panes, and one night there must have been a great gale for the window rattled, wind roared in the chimney and the whole house seemed to shudder under the buffeting of the wind. At other times I was aware of the sun on my face and the room was pervaded with a gentle warmth.

I remember looking down on the terrace and seeing Elizabeth and Gordon arrive in the open carriage with Parsons on the box. Joseph was there to receive them, handing down his daughter as though she were a queen. He spoke gaily and his voice sounded boyish.

'I hope that Parsons did not arrive too early for you? We wanted to make your stay as long as possible, didn't we, Florence?'

Florence was hidden from my view and her reply was inaudible.

The nursery was empty and cheerless and I watched greedily, determined to miss nothing. I knew that on this last day I was, for the time at least, excluded. Mechanically I walked to the door and stood looking at it, but I knew that it would not open for Brian Kenyon. I pulled my chair close to the window and sat staring out into the park. Eventually they came out, Charles and Elizabeth, and went down the steps by the ornamental pond; they stopped by the pond and it seemed that Elizabeth never ceased talking, while Charles gave me the impression of being quiet and withdrawn. After a moment or two they continued down the path and Elizabeth took his arm.

'What is the matter, Charles?'

'Nothing. What should be the matter?'

'Are you not glad to have me back, if only for a couple of days?'

'Of course I am glad to have you back.'

We are in the shrubbery, walking along the gravelled path towards the waterfall.

'Elizabeth . . .'

'Yes, Charles?' She looks at me with a smile which is coquettish as well as affectionate.

'When is the baby due?'

'There is no baby, Charles.'

'But . . .'

'There is no baby.'

'Have you told father?'

'No, and neither will you; not for the present.'

We walked on in silence, out on to the rock platform, down the steep path and past the maze.

'You said to me once, Charles, that if we remained single we could live together and I could keep house for you. I asked you if that would be enough and you said that you would make it so.'

'And so I would have done.'

She squeezes my arm and laughs. 'I have no doubt that you would—with frequent visits to the nearest Molly Couch. But what would have become of me?'

'Elizabeth!'

'Don't be a hypocrite, Charles!'

We walk through the wood and come out into the cove. It is half-tide and coming. We scramble over the rocks to the little sandy spit from which I usually bathe. Elizabeth stands looking up at the rocky chimney which, as children, we used to climb.

'I remember being halfway up there, petrified by fear.'

I cannot bear to be reminded of my dominating cruelty. 'I'm sorry.'

She turns quickly. 'No, Charles, you taught me something which

I have not forgotten—that men and women are not so very different, it is only custom which makes them seem so.'

We search for flat stones and send them skimming and bouncing across the water.

After a little while she says, 'You had your solution to our problem, Charles; I have found another. Gordon will be entirely happy with the bank and his little visits.'

'His visits?'

She has her back to me, bending over a clump of seaweed, separating the fronds in search of animals.

'Don't be such a simpleton, Charles! When Gordon looks at me he sees the bank's monogram, B.C.R., stamped on my forehead. That might arouse his passion but I never shall. He prefers his women plump and buxom.'

I say nothing; I dare not.

She is silent for a while, examining the brown, slimy fronds, then she straightens up and turns to me, looking steadily into my eyes as though with a challenge. 'Gordon and I have an arrangement, Charles, and you should be the last person to complain.'

Perhaps she senses the reason for my continuing silence, for when she speaks again her manner is unusually aggressive. 'I have to live in a man's world, Charles, but at least I shall do so on my own terms.'

I reach out impulsively for her hand. 'Don't let us quarrel.'

She smiles and kisses me. 'Dear Charles!'

We walk back to the house in silence until we are coming out of the shrubbery on to the lawn. 'Tell me one thing . . .'

'Yes, Charles?'

'On that night before your wedding . . .'

'Yes?'

'Did you know then that you were not pregnant?'

Her voice hardens. 'Don't interrogate me, Charles! In any case, what does it matter now?'

On the terrace she catches my arm. 'We have our lives in front of us, Charles . . .'

We sit round the table for luncheon; my father, aunt Florence, Elizabeth, Gordon and I.

'Will you take a little wine and water, Florence?'

'Thank you, no, Joseph.'

'Elizabeth? A little Chablis with water would do you no harm.'

'No, thank you, father.'

'No need to ask you, Gordon!' He laughs with great geniality. 'I know that you have a weakness for my hock. What about you, Charles?'

'No, father. No wine for me, thank you.'

Is it impossible for me to make myself agreeable?

'The hock, Richards.'

During the meal father has eyes only for Elizabeth, and she is at her most charming and vivacious. As he watches her, who can doubt his love? It is on her that he pins all his hopes. In his eyes she has just made a suitable match with a young man who, despite certain shortcomings, will be a pillar of the family business, something which I can never be. What if they did set tongues wagging by anticipating their wedding night? He has only to look at her to be convinced of her happiness. Together they must seem to him some compensation for a son whose callous indifference to all that he values is a continuing source of grief.

Never have I felt so great a tenderness toward him, poor deluded man that he is.

He will never know that his beloved daughter has had an incestuous relationship with her brother; that she has exploited her cousin's greed to contrive a loveless marriage as the price of an equivocal freedom. And who will tell him that his new son-in-law, agreeable and deferential as always, has sold himself as a complaisant husband?

Aunt Florence is watching me, and I have the absurd notion that she can read my thoughts. Certainly she has always come nearest to understanding me, and that is why I have hated her.

'Your father will destroy himself for you ungrateful children . . . It disgusts me, and I blame you for most of it.' That was what she said on the morning when we were left alone in the drawing-room while father broke the news to the Clarks. And she was right.

'Shall you visit your parents this afternoon, Gordon?'

'They will expect us, sir.'

'Then of course you must go. Parsons will drive you over.'

As they are leaving Elizabeth calls out to me: 'I shall be back before six, Charles!'

My father has said: 'Elizabeth is a remarkable young woman, Charles, with great strength of character . . . I do not condone what has happened; what I am saying is that she will overcome her difficulties and make a success of her marriage if she is allowed to.'

He was saying, 'Leave her alone.'

He could still be right.

I am perfectly calm. I go upstairs to the old nursery where there is now only one table. Her easel has gone also and the bookshelves are sparsely filled. Only her framed watercolours remain.

'Now you can make it a man's room, Charles!'

I am not in the least apprehensive or excited; on the contrary I feel unusually detached so that I can watch myself doing the things I have decided upon with a certain wonder at their futility.

I spend the afternoon destroying papers which I do not wish to be seen. I retrieve my journal from beneath the floorboards and burn it, page by page. Afterwards I take the trouble to gather all the ash in a bag and push it up the chimney. For some strange reason I am determined to leave no evidence of how I have spent these hours.

Such things attended to I remove my clothes and put on only a shirt, an old pair of trousers and rope shoes—the things I often wear when I go to bathe at the cove. No-one who sees me will think it unusual.

I am ready.

But at this point I hear the carriage returning although it is only five o'clock. I am concerned, even now my plan could fail. Out of my window I see Elizabeth being handed down by Gordon. They do not speak, and she goes off into the house, the carriage drives away, and Gordon is left standing on the terrace. It is evident that they have quarrelled. If Elizabeth comes into the nursery . . .

Gordon strolls down the steps and across the park looking like a

167

fat schoolboy in a pique. It is going to be more difficult than I had supposed.

But Elizabeth does not come to the nursery. I creep out into the corridor and steal along to the stairs like a thief. There is no-one about, I have rarely known the house so quiet. Through the hall and out on to the terrace. The park is still, as though waiting, and there is no-one in sight. I keep a sharp look-out for Gordon, I could not bear to meet him now. Through the shrubbery and out on to the rock platform; down the slope. The waterfall seems to be louder than usual though there cannot be a great quantity of water in this summer weather. Past the maze and down through the copse to the kissing-gate. I feel no wrench at leaving all this. Am I really and truly aware of what I am doing?

I think so.

Providence is with me, the cove is deserted, even Molly's door is closed; the water is like the proverbial mill-pond. I scramble over the rocks to the cove, concerned that Gordon might be there, but there is nobody, only a fishing boat far out to sea.

A quarter of a mile from the shore a strong current scours the bay for two or three hours after high-water. I do not undress for I do not want my clothes to be found. The water feels warm though not as welcoming as when I enter it naked. My trousers and shoes drag but I make progress, it is not far and there is no need to hurry. Swimming slowly and purposefully I draw away from the shore and in deeper water it seems easier. It is an hour-and-a-half after high-water and the current will be running most strongly . . . I do not look back and I have only a vague idea of how far I have come.

When I am in the current I shall not need to swim any more, only drift and I shall be carried far, far out to sea. I do not think that my body will be found.

Was it wrong and cruel of me not to write to Elizabeth?

CHAPTER TWELVE

I CAME TO myself standing by the pool at the foot of the water-fall; it was dark and raining hard, and I had no idea how I had got there. I was soaked to the skin and cold, every joint ached and my head throbbed. I realised that I must get back to the house or risk collapsing in the open. Climbing the steep path to the rock platform required a mammoth effort but I succeeded, though at the top I had to support myself against the tree, feeling dizzy and faint. I think that I must have passed out more than once on my way back to the house, and I remember sitting for what seemed a long time on the terrace steps, my back against one of the giant urns. But in the end I reached the plank door and let myself in.

The next thing I remember is making a frantic effort to light a fire, scooping out the dead wood-ash with my hands. Fortunately there was plenty of paper and wood, and I made a fire which blazed up and soon began to raise steam from my sopping clothes. I undressed, put on my pyjamas and wrapped myself in whatever else I could find, then I sat, huddled over the fire, until the heat scorched my cheeks and I was forced to move back. That is the last thing I remember before I woke in hospital.

I saw the chintz pattern of the curtains round my bed and the aluminium rod from which they hung, and above that the white ceiling. I knew instantly where I was, which makes me think that I had been asleep rather than unconscious. I was relieved; my last memory was of the nursery at Tregear where I lay in front of the fire without the strength to move. I closed my eyes again.

The next time I opened them there was a nurse bending over

me; she was young and pretty and dark; she reminded me of Elizabeth.

'What's wrong with me?'

'You'll live.'

They told me later that I had been in hospital for only two or three hours, and that I had been found lying on the floor in front of a fire which had burned itself out.

'Who found me?'

'A girl who lodges in the same house as you do—Karen somebody.'

I repeated my original question: 'What's wrong with me?'

'You're suffering from exposure and lack of food.'

In the evening Karen came to see me and we held hands but neither of us said much. When it was time for her to go she kissed me, and after she was gone I realised that I had not even thanked her.

For another day I lay in a semi-comatose condition, drifting between sleeping and waking, then I began to feel better, to sit up, take notice and eat more or less normal food. As I recovered bodily strength I also recovered my preoccupation with Tregear, with Charles and Elizabeth. I searched my memory to recall every incident through which I had seemed to live, every scrap of information I had gleaned. I was like the traditional miser with his hoard, counting out his coins, putting them into piles, rearranging them over and over again—anything for the sheer pleasure of handling them. It was an exercise which occupied most of my waking hours, and I resented the time I was forced to devote to hospital routine and to treatment—or the discussion of treatment.

It did not take the hospital people long to decide that my problem was of the mind, and I began to receive visits from a species of being I have since come to know well—the hospital psychiatrist, who can be either male or female (the female is the more deadly, for she refuses to admit that the game has any rules).

On the third day I was out of bed, and on the fourth I was persuaded to come to this place where I have now been for three months; much of that time spent in writing this account.

I put the final instalment of typescript on the shaman's desk. 'That's the lot.'

He picked up the little wad. 'I must say you've done this extremely well, Brian, it makes fascinating reading.' He laughed, showing his white teeth which seemed too many for his jaw. 'I'm sorry that this is the end of it.' He turned the pages. 'When I've read this we must get together for a long chat.'

'I'm leaving.'

'Leaving?' He looked shocked.

'I'm free to leave, surely?'

'Of course, but we're just beginning to get down to real treatment . . .'

'Karen is coming after lunch, I rang her this morning.'

He wanted to argue but I refused to let him. 'I've made up my mind.'

He fiddled with his red beard. 'I think you're making a big mistake, Brian.'

'Probably.'

'You will leave me your typescript?'

'I've got a copy.'

'If you want help you won't hesitate to get in touch?'

'No, it's very good of you.'

'You will have to discharge yourself.'

'Of course.'

He hesitated. 'Have you any money, Brian?'

'I think so, the county will have paid my salary—or part of it —into the bank.'

Karen arrived at half-past two, driving my Mini. I came out with a suitcase in one hand and my portable typewriter in the other.

'I hope you know what you're doing, Brian.'

'It's good of you to fetch me.'

She frowned. 'Go to hell!'

We were silent for the first two or three miles, then she said: 'Clarice has killed the fatted calf or something.'

'Oh God!'

'You'd better look pleased; you owe something to your friends.'

So I looked pleased and we spent an evening eating too much

and drinking quantities of Clarice's port. At half-past ten she said: 'You ought to be in bed, Brian, you need plenty of rest.'

The next day was Sunday and I was up early, before anyone else. I made some coffee, let myself out by the front door and coasted the Mini down the drive. There was every promise of a hot July day but the town was still deserted. I reached St Martin by eight and turned down the lane to the cove. I had the keys in my pocket, for, although Karen had returned the books and papers Clark had loaned me, nobody had said anything about the keys.

The cove was serene, the sea dazzling in the sunshine, and there was no-one about though there were three cars parked on the grass. I walked past the row of cottages to the kissing-gate, and felt that I was coming home. I let myself in and walked past the open woodshed, through the trees to the maze and the waterfall. Everything was as I had last seen it, except that now it was summer and everywhere foliage was denser and of a darker green. In the maze there were new shoots on the yew hedges. I wanted to stop everywhere and look at everything, but I kept on toward the house; through the shrubbery, across the lawn to the terrace, the steps, the urns, the nymph and the shuttered windows . . .

I walked round the house to the plank door and let myself in to the dim, cool kitchens; I went through the green baize door and up the stairs to the nursery. My packing-case and chair were still there and the grate was full of ash. I went over to the window and stood looking down at the park.

There were so many questions still to be answered, gaps to be filled. Charles had lived through every minute of every hour for twenty years and I had shared in only a tiny fraction of that time. I had no more idea now than I had before what combination of circumstances was necessary for me to make contact, but I was not concerned for now I had faith.

The change, when it came, was almost imperceptible, like the transition from waking to sleep.

The trees in the park were bare, the sky was a uniform pale grey, almost white. Near the window where I stood I could feel the chill as though the glass panes had been made of ice crystals. But when I turned to the room it was warm and welcoming. The nursery was as I had first seen it furnished, with pictures stuck to the walls and toys scattered around. A fire burned in the grate, protected by a guard. The two children were there, looking slightly older than on that first afternoon. Elizabeth sat on a low chair by the fire working at some embroidery, while Charles wandered about the room with an air of boredom.

'Read me some more of Mr Dickens's book, Charles.'

'If you like.'

I go over to the bookcase and reach down *A Tale of Two Cities*. I open the book at a marker, then, perched on the arm of her chair, I start to read:

'Chapter twenty-one. The chapter is called *Echoing Footsteps*.

'A wonderful corner for echoes it has been remarked, that corner where the doctor lived . . .'